APOCALYPSE SUMMER

Apocalypse Summer

This is a work of fiction. Names, characters, places, and incidents either are the product of the author's imagination or are used fictitiously. Any resemblance to actual persons, living or dead, events, or locales is entirely coincidental

Copyright © 2021 Tyler H. Jolley

Cover Design and Interior Layout by Melissa Williams Design

All rights reserved.

Published in the United States by Tyler H. Jolley

ISBN: 978-1-7331821-3-3

APOCALYPSE SUMMER

Tyler H. Jolley
Mary H. Geis

For Keaton, thank you for being my sounding board and for all the brain-
storming sessions that you let me put you through.
And thank you to the 80's for being so rad.

CHAPTER 1

A frantic hand slapped a round portal window, jarring Matt Voorhees awake for the first time in many years. He wiped crusty gunk from his eyes and blinked wildly. His surroundings should have been familiar, though he had no idea how much time had passed. Gray padding lined his oval cryopod and was supposed to give it a calming tone. He tried sitting up, but he only succeeded in tearing the feeding tube out of his belly button.

"Ah!"

Blood pooled in the fresh wound. He shook his head, trying to get his bearings, hand pressed hard against his stomach, his heart beating in his ears. Now unencumbered, he peered out the small viewport. A muscular boy with blond hair and striking deep-gray eyes stared back at him, yelling something and pawing at the lid to Matt's cryopod. Matt pressed his ear against the window.

"What?" Matt yelled. "I can't hear you!"

The boy's jaw slacked; his shoulders rolled forward,

then a thin, yellow substance forcefully hurled out of his mouth, covering the window.

Matt jerked back as if he was in the splash zone. His free hand landed on something plastic.

A VHS tape.

His face twisted in confusion. Even in the dim light he could make out at least half a dozen black tapes littering his pod. He tried to suck in a breath, but the air felt thick and old.

"I can't breathe!" Matt banged on the roof, hoping it'd budge. "Get me out of here! Hurry!" He scratched at his neck.

Not even his forceful kicks could jar the lid's seal. His chest heaved with struggling breaths. Sweat dotted his brow.

Thud!

Thud!

Thunk!

Matt peered through the vomit-covered viewport once more. The blond boy held a heavy tree branch like a baseball bat and swung, rattling the entire pod. His tan tank top—official uniform of the Save the Population Project—clung to him. Muscles bulged each time he swung the weapon. Bits of bark and splinters flew off, landing on the view window.

"Yes!" Matt yelled at him. He angled himself to get the most leverage and pressed against the top with his knees. His gut seared with pain.

Matt doubled over, clenching his stomach. Crimson liquid erupted like a volcano. The last time he'd felt that kind of pain, a girl had kneed him in the family jewels.

Saliva gathered under his tongue. His stomach lurched, but Matt swallowed hard. Bile burned his throat like he was drinking fire.

He rubbed a frustrated hand over his buzz cut, smearing his head with blood.

Then the idea clicked.

There had to be a latch somewhere inside the pod.

His hands reached blindly onto the smooth edges. He pulled back the fabric, desperate to find a seam or handle, his only source of light now stained and cracked. Shadows danced across the viewport. Matt shook his head.

"Come on, figure it out!" he said to himself.

The air felt thin, tasted empty, and his vision clouded.

He fell back into his seat and waited for darkness to take him.

A burst of light stunned him, two hands grabbed the front of his skintight uniform, and the blond boy dragged him onto the cool ground.

Before thanking him, Matt asked, "Did we make it? Did we survive the apocalypse?"

CHAPTER 2

"I ain't got a clue," the boy replied. "Get up, you gotta help! There are others."

"Where are we?" Matt yelled.

"Your guess is as good as mine." He held out his hand and pulled Matt to his feet. "Name's Cody."

"Matt." He scanned the area. "What the—what happened?"

In front of him, a green army-issued cargo truck sat cockeyed. Burnt rubber still lingered in the air. Strips of the blown-out tire and shattered pieces of solar panels lay on top of leaves. In the back of the truck was carnage. Like a toppled pile of stones, scratched and dented egg-shaped plastic cryopods spilled out of the canvas-covered bed.

Matt shook his head, taking in the scene. Fully grown, large trees shadowed the heavy layer of pine needles covering the ground.

"Forest?" Matt questioned. "Where are we?"

No answer. Cody was busy arming himself with the thick tree branch he'd used to crack open Matt's cryopod.

"Grab a stick, help me. Could you breathe in there?"

"No, not really," Matt said, still trying to make sense of all of it. "I mean, I guess I don't know. I felt like I was suffocating, but I think I was panicked."

"I don't know how much time we have," Cody said.

"Wait, how'd you get out?" Matt's stomach fluttered.

"Him." Cody pointed. A pair of crushed legs peeked out from under a smattering of pods behind the truck. Just like the Wicked Witch of the East under Dorothy's house. Blood slowly saturated the ground around him. "He got me out and said to help. Then he went to get another pod off the vehicle and then . . . I don't know. I guess they all tumbled. Crushed him. I tried to pull them off, but I couldn't do it by myself. So I opened yours. We gotta save him!"

Before Matt could react, the bile he'd forced down came up without warning.

"There ain't no time for that!" Cody yelled. He waved Matt toward him.

Lightheaded, Matt stood on the opposite side of a pod. "On three!" Matt yelled. "One, two, three." His voice strained on three.

Inside, a girl desperately pounded on the round window. Her muffled screams and tear-stained face begged for a way out.

"Hang on." Matt placed his hand on the viewport and turned to Cody. "We need to get her out. It's too heavy with her in it."

Matt again searched the edge for a latch or handle.

"Back up," Cody said, wielding a branch.

A dirt road next to the truck was lined with large rocks. Matt had seen similar paths for hiking when he was in the Scouts. He ran over and picked up a heavy, smooth rock. When he returned, Cody had busted a hole in the seam and had shoved in two thinner branches to pry it open. It was large enough for Matt to get a proper grip and lift. The plastic groaned under his weight and finally snapped open.

"Thank you," the girl gasped.

"Be still," Cody said. "We need to take out your feeding tube."

Although her hair was matted with sweat, the long black curls reminded Matt of a singer from *before*. *What was her name? She only had one name. Why can't I think of it?*

"Cher," he blurted out.

"Catherine." She wrinkled her nose at him. "Did you just call me Cher?"

"No. I mean yes. Are you okay?" Matt asked.

"I'm so confused. I feel sick. Are *you* okay?" She pointed to his stomach and blood-smeared face.

"Fine. It's fine. Look, you'll probably puke. We both did. Here." He offered her a hand, then slipped on the crushed man's blood.

She screamed. "What is that?"

"We'll fill you in later, but we need to get all of these open," Cody said.

Matt grabbed one side of the empty pod, and Cody did the same and nodded at him. They heaved it like a sack of potatoes and threw it aside, revealing a smashed arm beneath.

"We have to get the rest off him," Matt said. "We have to save him!"

Catherine returned with a bundle of sticks. Her uniform had the number *17* on the left breast of her tank top, same as her pod.

"Okay," Matt said. "Cody, hit that side; I'll use my rock on the other. Catherine, when one of us breaks the seam, put the sticks in and pry it open."

"No," she said. "There has to be a better way."

"Unless you got a better plan, we're gonna do this," Cody said.

Every smack of the rock sent shock waves up Matt's arms and into his spine. He pounded and pounded on the same spot until a hole formed. "Bring me some sticks," he yelled.

Catherine pushed a thick branch into the void and pressed down on the end like it was a teeter-totter. "I've got this. Go to the next one," she said.

Matt looked down at his own bloody wound and said, "Don't forget about the feeding tube."

"I need some help, y'all," Cody called out.

A boy, over six feet tall, stumbled out of the pod. Matt helped Cody slide the final pod off the old man. Long, wiry gray hair a shade darker than his equally long, frizzy beard was matted in the coagulated pool of blood. Coke-bottle lenses had been smashed into his face and were embedded in the skin over his orbital bones. His body looked flat, too flat under his white lab coat. Blood seeped out of every orifice. There was no saving him.

They were on their own.

CHAPTER 3

"He's dead," Cody said.

"Who the heck is he?" Matt asked, putting hands on his hips.

Catherine pointed to the pods. Faces filled the portholes, banging and screaming against them. "There's no time to waste. They're running out of air! Let's figure out who he is later."

"She's right," Matt said. He picked up a new rock.

"There must be a more efficient way to do this," Catherine said.

"If you find a way, let me know." Cody abruptly turned and continued his assault on the cryopods.

Somehow, in all the chaos, Matt hadn't noticed Cody's heavy southern accent until now. A memory of meeting him *before* flashed through his mind. He pressed his palms into his eyes. *No, not now.*

Between people hitting the inside of their pods and the three teenagers breaking into them, Matt was sure they'd draw some attention and, more importantly, help.

Next to him, the tall boy Cody had freed stood shell-shocked, holding his gut.

"Grab a rock or a branch," Matt said. "Help us get them out."

"My name is Justin," he replied. He stared forward, unmoving.

Matt pointed to the pile of cryopods in the back of the truck and the ones scattered on the ground. "Fine, whatever, just get something to wedge these open."

Justin's sandy-blond hair stuck to his sweaty forehead. He blinked but said nothing.

"What's your damage?" Matt shook Justin's shoulders, immediately regretting it. Up close, he realized that Justin not only towered over him but was also strong, more muscular than Matt had initially realized. "Snap out of it!"

Justin brushed Matt's hands off him. He dropped to his knees and held his head. "Sorry, I—I'm just a little dizzy."

This time, Matt ignored him and returned to his task at hand. Justin was either going to help or not. But babysitting him wasn't an option. Matt lifted the heavy, smooth rock overhead and brought it down as hard as he could. The humid air didn't satisfy his thirsty lungs as he worked. His fingers bled, but he hardly noticed.

"I got one," Cody yelled.

"Over here! Me too," Catherine said.

"That fast?" Matt turned. "How? Oh man, Catherine, are you okay?"

Blood covered Catherine's hands and feet. It was

smeared up to her arms, and splatters dotted her thighs and tan-colored shorts.

"I found a key," she said, "on the dead guy. I knew there was an easier way. Every problem has a solution. I'll unlock, you pull them open."

"Rad," Matt said.

The old man was now facedown. His belt had been pulled free of his body and lay next to him like a dead snake. A small coin purse had been carelessly emptied onto the soft, bloody dirt. Chapstick, a Swatch with a colorful band, and a utility knife were strewn about.

Catherine stepped from pod to pod, locating the inconspicuous lock flush with the plastic. Matt wondered how she had even found it in the first place.

The airtight lid hissed as Matt lifted it. A beautiful girl with blond hair sobbed.

"Get it out! Get it out! Get it out!" She pointed at her stomach.

"Okay, just stay still. Justin," Matt yelled at him, "we need your help, now!"

Matt carefully held the feeding tube. The girl grabbed his arm. "No, not you. Look at your stomach. I can't have a scar!"

"Your belly button is already a scar."

"Don't touch me!" she hissed.

"Then stay still until someone can unhook you!" Matt yelled more forcefully than he'd intended.

By now Catherine had unlocked all but one pod. Justin and Cody had opened most of them and unhooked their respective feeding tubes. *This is going to be Barf City in a few minutes.*

Matt ran toward Catherine. The lush forest and trees caught his attention for a moment, but he turned his focus back to Catherine. She struggled with the heavy lid but had it propped open a few inches. Matt shoved his hand into the void and lifted with all his might.

A small girl with porcelain skin lay in the fetal position; a dark bruise had formed on her temple, her dark-brown hair a sweaty, tangled mess. Matt tugged on her shoulder. The number 7 was embroidered on the left breast of her tank top. He jerked his hand back as if he'd touched something hot, then immediately closed the pod.

"We're too late, aren't we?" Catherine asked.

"No, it wasn't our fault," Matt said. "She's already cold. It was probably from the impact when the truck blew a tire. We couldn't have saved her." *I think.*

By now, most of the freed teenagers had gathered around them.

Catherine turned to the group. "We lost one. It's a damn shame. She lived through the cryofreeze only to die in a car accident. Let it be a lesson to us all. Safety is of the utmost importance."

"Who do you think you are?" Justin asked. "The spokesperson for us? You sure as shit don't represent me. For all we know, you killed her."

"What?" Catherine took an involuntary step backward. "I found the key. I *saved* most of you."

"Not me," Justin said. "That hick did. Hey, hick, where'd you get that accent?"

"Texas." Cody stared at the ground. A muscle ticked in his jaw. "This ain't helping nothin.'"

"Oh, it *ain't?*" Justin crossed his arms, a smirk plastered on his face.

"Look, everyone needs to calm down," Matt said. "Let's all get reacquainted—it's been a minute since we all met, and that was only for a short time before we were cryogenically frozen. Then we'll figure out what to do as a *group*. And yes, Catherine is the one who found the key. If not for her, we'd still be smashing in lids, trying to get you guys out. Who knows if your air would have lasted that long?"

Justin's shoulder's relaxed. Everyone else stared at Matt. *I guess I'm the leader, for now.*

"Um, hello?" a girl called out. "Hey, butt-face, you forget about me? Get me out of here, like now!"

CHAPTER 4

Matt leaned his head back and blinked hard. The blond who didn't want a scar in her scar. He had forgotten about her.

"Can someone please help her?" Matt asked.

"*Her* is Kim," the girl said.

Matt put a palm to his forehead.

"You just left her?" Catherine asked, walking toward Kim.

"She wanted someone else to help her with her feeding tube."

"I see," Catherine said. She reached into the pod. "I'll help you."

"No," Kim said, pointing to a huge guy. "I want him."

The boy lumbered over and gently caressed Kim's stomach. "Me? Little ol' me?" His initial smirk was now a full-on, smug smile.

I bet he used to be a jock.

"Puh-weese," Kim pouted. She actually stuck out her bottom lip.

He bent down and kissed her full lips, then pulled the tube from her stomach. "I never thought I'd see you again." He lifted her up and hugged her, and she wrapped her legs around his waist.

"Get a room," someone said.

"Gag me with a spoon," said another.

"Looks like they don't need reacquainting," Catherine said under her breath.

"Yes, we do. Like, all night long." Kim giggled.

"Okay, let's form a circle," Matt said, ignoring the PDA.

They all wore skintight, tan Save the Population Project uniforms. There was a light-blue number over the breast of each uniform.

"We'll go around and reintroduce ourselves one by one. I'm Matt Voorhees. I'm from—I was from Nevada, and like the rest of you from our cryocolumn, I'm seventeen. Last I knew it was the summer of 1985. I love movies, and I love quoting them even more."

"Voorhees?" a redheaded girl said. "Like from those horror movies?" She scrunched her nose.

"Yes! Exactly. Love that show," Matt said. *Maybe I shouldn't have mentioned my love of movies.*

He nodded for Cody to go next.

"Cody Anderson, Texas. That's where I got my *hick* accent from."

"Okay, okay, sorry." Justin held up his hands. "Maybe we got off on the wrong foot. I was just a little confused at first. Sorry, man."

"Apology accepted." Cody nodded.

"I'm Stacy King," the redhead said. "I obviously have strawberry-blond hair, and it's my favorite accessory." She twisted a frizzy curl. "And if anyone knows how to give perms, speak up, because I'm probably overdue."

"Looks red to me," Kim said.

"It's strawberry-blond." Stacy's eyes squinted, and her lips formed an angry, straight line.

"I'm Victoria Stewart," a petite girl said. She hugged herself with slender arms. Her long black hair was stick straight and cascaded down to the middle of her back. Black eyeliner had been smudged, and it looked like she had been crying. "I'm from Manhattan. My hobbies include getting the hell back to New York. Where are we?"

"I don't know." Matt shook his head. "What else?"

"I also like the arts," she meekly replied to Matt.

"I'm not sure *The Goonies* qualify as 'the arts,' but I think we can find some common ground." Matt offered her a smile.

"Kyle Owens. Hartford, Connecticut." The boy stood confidently, even though he was the shortest male of the group. His black hair was cut short, no-nonsense. "I'm a member of the Young Republican's National Federation. Alex P. Keaton is my hero, and I love to read. I was in the middle of the *Lord of the Rings* trilogy before I was called to go into cryosurvival with my family. So if you've finished the series, I'll ask kindly that you do not spoil it for me."

"Alex P. Keaton? Ha!" Kim laughed. "I'm Kim Baker. Okay, so like, I was and will always be a cheerleader. I grew up in Iowa, but I'm going to be a star in Hollywood. And this beefcake is Rhett." She pulled on his arm. He lowered his shoulder, and she kissed him on the cheek.

"Rhett Young. Washington. The state." He was the tallest of the bunch. Reminded Matt of a less muscular Hulk Hogan. "Would have been class of 1986 if we hadn't gotten frozen. Go Wild Cats! Woo-Woo!"

"Wait, how did you guys meet before this?" Victoria asked. "I mean, it's obvious you have a past."

"We met on the bus, the night before we were frozen. Had to go out with a bang, if you know what I mean." Kim smoothed her feathered hair.

Rhett smirked.

"Ew!" Victoria said.

"I think it's romantic." Stacy swooned.

"Enough of this," Kyle said. "We need to get down to business."

"What business, dork?" Kim asked. "The apocalypse is, like, obviously over. Chill."

"Chill? That's mental," Kyle said. "There's a dead female in a pod and a crushed elderly gentleman who was transporting us. For what? Huh? For what purpose? Where are we, and *when* are we? And where is the cryovault?"

CHAPTER 5

"Don't yell at her!" Rhett stood between Kim and Kyle. His deep voice echoed in the forest.

"Calm down, big guy." Justin placed a hand on Rhett's shoulder, guiding him back into the perimeter of the circle. "How tall are you anyway? Six-six?"

"Yup," he said, upper lip still twitching.

"Well, you got two inches on me, dude. Name's Justin's Lewis. Doesn't matter where I'm from, doesn't matter what I've done. I'm here, I have no fear, and I need a beer."

No one laughed.

Justin clapped once. "Not the response I was expecting. You guys need to calm down. Franky says relax!" He turned to a skinny boy the same height as him. It looked like he had hit puberty late and hadn't had a chance to fill out. "What's your name, kid?"

"Na-Nathan Mo-Mo-Moore. I'm from U-Utah." He turned his head to the side and whispered something into his hand. "So-sorry. I get a little nervous some-some-sometimes."

"It's okay," Catherine said. "I think we're all a little nervous. I'm Catherine Turner. I did gymnastics when I was a kid. I'd just started coaching elementary girls when we were recruited here."

"You're the one that found the key?" Stacy asked.

"Yes," she replied. "It was on the dead man's belt." Her curls had dried and were big and thick. She nervously tucked a section behind her ear.

"Gross." Stacy wrinkled her nose. "But thank you. You saved our lives."

"I couldn't have without Cody and Matt. They got me out to begin with."

"How did you get out first?" Justin crossed his arms and pointed to Cody and Matt with his chin.

"I was out first," Cody said. "The old man unsealed my pod and woke me. He was dang near frantic. Some-thin' about the truck wrecked, and a meltdown . . . I don't know, I was just tryin' to get my bearings. It happened so fast. He ran back to the truck, and there was a loud crash. I unhooked my feeding tube, and that's when I saw him crushed. Matt's was the closest cryopod to me, so I cracked it open. But I didn't have the key. Heck, I didn't *know* there was a key or how to open it. So I grabbed a branch and beat the sh—pardon me—the crap out of one until it opened."

"Who is he?" Rhett asked.

"I think he's the scientist," Catherine said. "I remember him. We met him the same day we all met. Right before we were frozen. He's so much older now. How long have we been gone?"

"You're right. That is him," Matt said. "But he's gotta be at least twenty years older. Maybe more."

"What?" Kim yelled. "Are you telling me that I, like, missed my twenties? I'm in my thirties? Almost"—she gagged—"forty!"

"No, you're still seventeen," Matt said. "Kim, stop crying! We didn't age. Time was suspended for us. Everything aged around us, but we didn't. Okay? That's how cryosleep works."

"I don-don't remember much of anything," Nathan said.

"Me neither," Stacy said.

"Sure you do," Victoria said. "The weather was destroying the earth, like some sort of apocalypse. Then a bunch of scientists got together and decided to detonate an H-bomb in the Mariana Trench to tilt the world's axis one degree. But all it did was boil a bunch of fish and mammals and prolong the inevitable." She shrugged. "Sorry, animal lover here."

"That's awfully shortsighted of you to say," Kyle said. "It did fix the weather—for a while."

"Oh really, Mr. Republican?" Victoria raised an eyebrow. "All they did was kill a bunch of defenseless whales and fish!" She was yelling at this point. "And some hypotheses are that they actually *sped up* the weather patterns."

"Here we go." Kyle pinched the bridge of his nose. "A conspiracy theorist."

"How are hundreds of thousands of cooked fish a

theory? I'd call that proof. The ocean died that day, and you know it. *Your* people caused it."

"My people?" Kyle took a step forward.

Matt grabbed Kyle's arm. "We all caused it. Now, everyone stop. What's happened is done. We were lucky, we were chosen in the lottery to live. Raise your hand if you are the only one from your family that was picked."

No one raised their hands.

"Okay, so we all have family. This is good," Matt said. "Now we just have to wait for them. Surely there'll be another truck coming with pods. We'll flag them down, and they'll send for help."

"I dunno, buddy," Cody said. "We've been here a good hour, and I haven't heard a peep from either direction."

"Someone has to know we're gone, right?" Catherine asked.

"Of course—I mean, I think," Matt said.

"What about over th-there?" Nathan asked.

"Where?" Victoria stared in the direction Nathan had pointed. She jumped twice, then said, "Please, pick me up, I'm only five-two. I don't have a good vantage point."

They gathered next to Nathan to see what he was talking about. Across the forest, they could barely make out a pitched rooftop.

"Is that a house?" Stacy asked.

"Um . . ." Victoria started. "Usually a house in the woods is called a cabin."

"That's true," Justin said. "It's a cabin."

"I think we should stay put," Matt said. "All my

Scout training says to stay in one place so you can easily be found."

"No way," Kim said. "Listen, I didn't survive the apocalypse to just sit on a roadside hoping for a ride, like a hitchhiker."

"Maybe there's a phone we can use down there," Cody suggested.

"True," Matt said.

"Who died and made you leader?" Justin asked. "Screw this. All in favor of heading to the cabin, follow me. Those who want to stay and eat dirt, go for it."

"Wait," Matt said. "We need to stick together. I relent. Yes, let's go to the cabin, but if there's no phone, we need to all agree to stay put for a few days, so when people come they'll find us."

"Whatever, chief," Justin said. "Let's go."

"Wait," Matt said. "Let's leave a note. And we need to bring the scientist and girl. They deserve a proper burial."

"I'll try to find something to write on," Catherine said.

"I'll see if there's some rope in the truck," Cody said. "I'm pretty dang good with knots. We can put them in the lid of the pods and drag them behind us."

"I'm not doing that," Stacy said.

"You won't have to," Kyle said. "The girl is still in her pod."

"Ugh, this is going to suck," Kim said. "We, like, don't even have shoes. I can't walk that far barefoot."

"It'll b-be fine," Nathan said.

"Speak for yourself," Stacy shot back, then she smirked at Kim.

"Found some!" Cody stood in the bed of the truck with rope above his head.

"Great. Let's get the man loaded up," Matt said.

Rhett and Kyle helped Cody with the ropes while Nathan placed the deceased scientist into a pod.

"We ready yet?" Justin asked.

"Yes," Matt said. "Wait! The tapes!"

CHAPTER 6

Matt tripped over a broken branch in the rush to retrieve the nine generic black VHS tapes that had been haphazardly placed in his pod. Cody followed him and took the ones Matt couldn't carry.

"What are these for?" Cody asked.

"I'm not sure. Did you have any in yours?" Matt said.

"I don't think so."

"I doubt I'm the only one with them." He turned back toward the group. "Guys, check to see if you have videos in your pods."

"Oh, great call." Justin rolled his eyes. "Then we'll just play them right . . . ah, crap! I forgot my VCR."

"Maybe there's a VCR at the cabin," Victoria said.

"Hold on." Kyle rummaged around, tearing out gray padding. "This is weird. At the temperatures we were kept at, the tapes would have shattered. No, this was done after we were removed from the cryovault and started to thaw."

Everyone froze.

"You're right." Matt rubbed the back of his neck. The prickly hairs on his neck tickled his palms. "Did anyone else have tapes or anything else in their pod?"

"No."

"Why you?" Justin asked.

Yeah, why me?

"I don't know." Matt deposited the precious videos into the pod with the girl, then pulled on one of the ropes. "Let's just get to the camp and out of the open space."

"Camp?" Stacy asked. "How do you know it's a camp, *Voorhees?*"

"Fine, cabin. Whatever." Despite the hot, humid air, a chill sent shivers down Matt's spine. "It doesn't matter. We need to leave."

"Something is wrong." Victoria closed her eyes and titled her head toward the sky. "The energy feels off. Does it feel creepy to anyone else?"

"The only creepy thing is Matt *Voorhees* taking us to a camp in the middle of nowhere." Stacy laughed. "Did you bring your hockey mask?"

Kim joined her in laughter. "You know, Stacy, I think we're going to get along just fine."

"Matt!" Catherine yelled.

He jogged to the passenger side of the truck. Catherine held her head in her hands, her shoulders hunched.

"What's wrong?" Matt heard footfalls behind him. Over his shoulder he saw Kim, Cody, and the others following his lead. He took another step toward Catherine.

A boy—no, man—lay slumped on the green Naugahyde seat. He wore the same tan uniform tank top and shorts as them, with the addition of a thick Everlast leather weight-lifting belt. Matt had seen athletes wear similar ones in the weight room at high school. His light-brown hair was to his shoulders and feathered, like Kim's. Almond eyes and an underdeveloped jaw revealed crowded teeth that poked out of his relaxed mouth.

"Is he . . ." Catherine whispered.

"Why is he so filthy?" Kim asked, looking down at her clean tan uniform.

Matt gingerly placed two fingers on the man's neck, expecting nothing but coldness. "No. He's got a pulse. It's strong." Matt shook the man's shoulders; his head flopped without resistance. "Hey mister, wake up."

"Maybe he's hurt?" Cody offered. "Probably shouldn't shake him much."

Matt gave the man a quick once-over—no obvious signs of head trauma or open wounds.

"I don't think so." Matt propped him back in the seat. "Maybe he's just passed out."

"Now what?" Stacy asked. "Ew, he's gross. Leave him."

"Are you crazy?" Kyle stepped up. "*Obviously*, we're not leaving him. Can someone help us?"

Kyle stomped off; Catherine followed. They returned with a heavy cryopod.

"If he's been in the truck this whole time"—Catherine wiped her brow—"then he knows where we are, right? He looks older than us."

"Maybe," Matt said. "But he's wearing the same uniform as us. It looks like he might be from another age column."

"But why's he out of his pod?" Justin asked.

"I don't know, let me ask him." Matt rolled his eyes. "Look, he was probably supposed to help the scientist lift our pods. See his belt? I'm guessing he passed out during the wreck."

"When's he gonna wake up?" Rhett asked.

"I have no idea. I literally have the same info as you," Matt snapped. "Nathan, can you help me move him? Justin, Cody, you two want to pull the scientist and the girl? We'll all swap out and take turns, okay?"

"Aye-aye, captain." Justin saluted him.

"Yes"—Nathan paused and bit his lip, suppressing a stutter—"I can help. Is your stomach okay?"

"I think so." Matt lifted his tank top to check his belly button. A soft clot had formed in the void. "Not bad."

They followed the dirt road toward the camp. The soft ground was unlike any dirt Matt had ever seen. Dark brown with red undertones. Tall redwoods towered over them. Lush green ferns and flowery bushes filled in the gaps between trees.

"I hate to be an ingrate, but I hope there are real clothes at this place." Victoria crossed her arms over her flat chest.

"What's wrong with these?" Kim frowned. "They're just like the bloomers we wear under our cheerleading skirts."

"Exactly," Victoria said. "They're undergarments. I'd never leave my apartment in a sports bra or shorts this tight. Not even in Manhattan."

"I think I grew when I was frozen," Rhett said. He took the ropes from Matt and Nathan and pulled the pod holding the unconscious man by himself. "Mine are too tight."

"Physically impossible, you big dumb animal," Kyle muttered too quietly for anyone but Matt to hear.

"Shh," Matt said. "Do you hear that?"

Silence.

"I think you're losing it, chief," Justin said. "I don't hear jack."

"Exactly," Matt said. "It's silent. We're in a forest, and we don't hear birds, insects, or anything. Not even rustling leaves from the wind. Victoria is right. It kinda feels sterile, or like something is lacking."

"Maybe the apocalypse killed them off?" Catherine said. "And it's a calm day. We should be thankful for that, given everything that happened."

"No way." Matt picked up his speed. "I've never seen a forest like this without a single animal. And how are the trees so big?"

"You need to take a chill pill," Kim said. "It's a new world. Post-apco whatever. We beat it, that's all that matters. Learn to live in the moment."

"I'm just trying to figure this all out, that's all," Matt said.

"N-no problem," Nathan said. "K-Kyle, should we take a turn?"

"Absolutely. We all need to contribute and pull our weight. Thanks for pulling this far." He took a rope from Justin.

"Wait," Catherine said. "Nathan, you rest, you've had a go already. I'll pull the girl; you get the scientist, Kyle."

"Ma'am." Cody tipped his imaginary cowboy hat at Catherine before giving her his rein. "Thank you much."

"Don't mention it."

Matt listened for sounds of life, anything to give him comfort, but all he heard was chatter amongst the other survivors. No insects, no birds. Nothing buzzed near his ear. He stared at the road. No creeping or crawling things. Something else was missing, but he couldn't put his finger on it at first. Then it dawned on him.

"Guys—"

"I'm a woman, thank you very much," Victoria said.

"Don't you think it's weird there aren't any tire tracks on the road?" Matt asked.

"Of course there are," Kyle said. "How else did they build the cabins?"

"But no *recent* tire tracks. They've eroded away," Matt said. "Seems like no one has been here for a while."

"All you do is focus on the weird stuff," Stacy said. "Look! There's the entrance. Let's go!"

CHAPTER 7

Matt walked through an archway. Tall wooden spires jutted high into the air, then gradually shortened one by one until they leveled out and formed the perimeter. A huge, rusted metal sign connected the two poles at the top, with the words *New Beginnings* painted on it. Paint had chipped away on the sign, giving their visit to Camp New Beginnings a haunting welcome. The panoramic backdrop was a lone snowcapped mountain. The single snowcapped peak was jagged.

"Is that the Matterhorn?" Matt asked.

"I don't know what kind of janky Disneyland you've been to, but this definitely isn't it," Kim said.

"News flash, Kim," Kyle said. "The Matterhorn is based off a real mountain in the Swiss Alps."

"Whatever," Kim said. "Wait, does that mean we're like, in Switzerland? My parents promised to take me on a European vacation when I graduated."

"I don't think so." Kyle pointed. "The Matterhorn has more of a spike at the top. That one is pretty rounded."

"Great, so you don't know where we are," Justin said. "Thanks for the history lesson."

"You mean geography," Catherine said.

"Yeah, yeah," Justin shrugged, "whatever."

Matt took a couple of steps forward. "Let's check it out."

Inside the grounds, the same reddish-brown dirt lined the pathways. But someone had taken care and lined them with glittery quartz rock. Pale pinks, whites, and a few purples glinted in the sunlight. In the middle of the camp, a huge main cabin loomed. Matt guessed it housed the mess hall and stage for plays, presentations, and performances. At least, that was how it had been at summer camps he'd attended. Beyond the main house were a dozen modest cabins. Untouched and overgrown with moss.

"Here's to our new beginning." Justin laughed. "How lame."

"Totally," Stacy said. "This new beginning is bogus."

Tall grass had overgrown in the areas between paths. The trees inside the camp weren't as large as the redwoods outside. Colorful bark like nothing he'd ever seen grabbed his attention. It reminded him of the story of his parents' honeymoon in Maui. His mom had fallen in love with the rainbow eucalyptus trees, and his dad was bound and determined to grow one for her at home. This led to many failed attempts and dead trees in their Nevada yard. His heart sank. *They'll find us. They have to.*

"I think I'll stay out here." Victoria splayed her arms out, head toward the sky, and turned in a circle. "I need to be one with the Earth. Get reacquainted with this new post-apocalyptic world."

"You can, soon." Matt scanned the area. The hair on his neck stood at attention. "We need to stick together. It seems like this place was abandoned, and I honestly don't know what that means for us."

"Even better—no adult supervision required." Rhett smirked.

"Hey, there's a lake," Kim said. On the far side of the cabin, beyond some overgrown ferns and grass, was a lake. "Let's swim."

"Pardon me, everyone." Cody stepped up onto the stairs in front of the building and faced everyone. "But Matt ain't wrong. We need to scope this place out first. Look for some help, find a phone or radio—"

"Who would we call?" Kyle asked.

"The Youn-Young Republican group?" Nathan folded his lips in, suppressing a laugh.

"Federation," Kyle corrected him.

They stared at each other for a moment before erupting into laughter.

Matt joined Cody on the creaky steps. "Let's get in there, find a VCR so we can see what the hell's going on, then bury these two. After that, whatever. Split up, do what you want. I'm done being the babysitter."

"Sorry," Victoria said. "I wasn't trying to be difficult. I'm just scared."

"M-m-me too," Nathan said. "I was just trying to tell a joke."

"It's fine, I get it. But let's do this as a team," Matt pleaded. "Okay?"

"Great, chief. Team New Beginnings." Justin walked past Matt and slapped him on the shoulder on his way up the stairs. "Go team, go!"

Matt gritted his teeth but stayed silent. *I will not stoop to his level.*

"What do we do with this one?" Kim pointed to the man resting in a pod. His chest rose and fell steadily. "I think we should name him. He looks like a Lance."

"Rude," Catherine said.

"That guy is better?" Stacy asked. "Lance it is."

Matt massaged the back of his neck as he climbed the stairs. "Let's make sure it's safe inside first, then we'll bring him in."

Red stain had chipped and worn away the wide staircase. Both railings, heavily warped and bowed, showed signs of water damage. The covered wraparound porch seemed better for the wear, though most of the planks had scratch marks, and the exposed wood had grayed over time. Tumbleweeds blocked the grand front doors.

"I'll take care of those." Catherine grabbed two of the straw-colored weeds and tossed them off the side. Nathan joined in and cleared the rest. "Thanks."

"Should we knock?" Cody asked. "Wouldn't be right to go bargin' into someone's home."

"I don't what kind of house you grew up in, Tex, but this isn't a home," Justin said.

Matt knocked despite Justin's comments, then turned the brass handle. The connection was loose, but it still clicked open. The termite-eaten door creaked loudly, announcing their arrival.

"Hello?" Matt stepped through the threshold.

The enormous A-frame room was lit only by the light flooding in through the tall windows. On the left side of the entrance was a stage that encompassed the length of the gym. Heavy, dust-covered, black curtains were tied back and exposed the depth of the stage. On the opposite wall was a huge floor-to-ceiling fireplace. Bricks had crumbled away in spots, revealing mottled cement. Peeled-up varnish on the hardwood floor exposed a basketball court, but the rims and backboards were retractable and currently faced the ceiling. Along the walls were roughly a hundred wooden folding chairs, stacked five to a spot.

"Guess they were into the arts too, Victoria," Matt said, his voice shaky.

"Let me see." She caught up to Matt and stood flush with him. "Huh, looks like the one we had at my school. Pretty standard. I'd like to get a closer look, see what type of lighting system they have. Any chance there's electricity?"

"Let's have a look." Cody flipped a switch.

"Dang," Matt said. "Nothing."

"That means no phone." Stacy's voice rose to a high pitch. "And that means no TV or VCR. Those tapes are probably just stupid home videos anyway." She paced. Her breath was so heavy, her entire chest cavity puffed up and deflated at an alarming rate. "We are stuck here. Where's here? The middle of nowhere, and no one knows we're here. We have nothing! Nothing at all. No malls, no fast food—food! What will we eat?"

"Stop it!" Kim slapped Stacy across her cheek. "Snap out of it!"

Stunned, Stacy held her cheek.

"I didn't think you'd be the first to crack," Kim said. "Get it together, like, now, Stacy, or I can't be associated with you."

"Guys"—Catherine pointed out the window—"what's that?"

CHAPTER 8

Matt paused, giving someone else the chance to confront whatever Catherine saw. Everyone was a tough guy until it came down to brass tacks. Matt rolled his eyes and approached the smudged window.

"What?" he asked.

"That." Catherine pointed.

A ripped blue tarp covered a construction-yellow rectangle. The word *CAT* was visible from the tear in the plastic.

"I think that might just be our salvation for the night. Cody, come with me. Everyone else, search the place for a TV and VCR. It's probably going to be in one of the nearby rooms. If you find one, bring in the tapes. Oh, and grab some of the chairs and set them up, okay?"

"Whatever, chief," Justin said. He ran a hand through his messy hair.

"Can a few of you bring Lance up here?" Matt ignored Justin, again, and exited the building, Cody in tow.

"What did you see?" Cody asked.

"I don't want to jinx it. Let's look before I say anything more."

Matt ran down the stairs, gripping the railing, then toward the side of the building. Rhett and Nathan followed after them but stopped at Lance's pod.

Old, rotten leaves crunched under Matt's feet. With each step he unleashed their musty, mildewy scent. He kicked branches, garbage, and pine needles out of his way to fully expose the tarp. Crusty and frayed bungee cords weakly held the plastic in place over the machine. He pulled it free and exposed it.

"Yes!" Matt fist-pumped toward the sky. "It's a generator. It's huge, I've seen cars smaller than this bad boy." He slapped the side of it; something inside the machine rattled. "I think it's commercial-sized, like what they have at hospitals. And look! It's been retrofitted for the apocalypse. Rad."

On the back of the generator was a bicycle seat, pedals, and handlebars. Below it, an old oil puddle had stained the ground with chips of yellow paint on top, like confetti.

"What's the bike for?" Cody asked. "I'm a decent mechanic, but I ain't never seen nothin' like this."

"I've seen this in my techie magazines. But they were just ideas; I didn't know it was real. You pedal the bike, and it charges the batteries. Once it has enough stored-up charge, the generator runs, no gas required. This is new stuff. Like high tech. Who were these people?" Matt asked. He rubbed his hand over his short hair, then stared at his hand. Dried blood had flecked off onto his palm.

"I didn't want to be rude, but maybe you should wash that blood off your face and head," Cody said.

"Sure, yes. After this. Let's give it a try," Matt said.

Matt walked around to the covered control panel. A rusted silver lever fought with him, but he cranked it up and revealed the inner workings. "See this key?" A small, white rubber keychain dangled from it. "It turns over just like a car ignition. Once I've pedaled for a few minutes, fire it up and we'll give it a try."

"Should we get others out here to take turns?" Cody asked.

"Not yet. I don't want to get their hopes up until we know it still works."

As he climbed onto the machine and settled onto the uncomfortable seat, Matt was flooded with flashbacks. Riding down the street with his friends had been his favorite pastime when he was young kid. They'd attach discarded playing cards from local casinos in between the spokes with clothespins and whir around, pretending they were on motorcycles. Once they got older, they'd ride out to the desert. Wrecking on sand was preferred over asphalt. Building jumps and roller tracks. Summers seemed endless when Matt was on a bike.

His feet settled onto the pedals like an experienced rider. The chains cranked to life, slow and angry at first. After a few revolutions, the dirt and rust had given way to a smoother ride. The handlebars were old, like from a Mongoose pit bike. It felt right. Normal. It was a weird juxtaposition: the world had mostly died, and here he was, riding a "bike" like nothing had happened.

"Matt," Cody called. "Where'd you go, buddy?"

"Huh?" he shook the cobwebs from his head. His legs felt like jelly. The smell of hot oil wafted into his nose.

"I've been calling your name for five minutes. You were somewhere else. Thought I was gonna have to shake you."

"Just remembering how it was before. I loved biking. My parents got after me for watching too many movies, so they bought me a bike to get me out of the house. It became my second favorite thing to do."

"Never been much of a cyclist myself," Cody said. "Do you think it's okay to try the gennie?"

"Go for it." Matt pulled his feet back and let the pedals slow on their own to a stop. He panted and wiped his brow with his forearm, smudging the newly moistened blood.

Cody grasped the key, took a deep breath, and turned it to the right. The machine sputtered, then moaned. The moaning started strong, then slowly dissipated and grew weaker by the second. Eventually it lost all hope and gave way to a steady *click, click, click.*

"Not enough," Cody said. "You want me to give it a ride? Take a break?"

"No." Matt pulled off his tank top. The number *20* on the breast side flashed by his face as he yanked it over his head. "Give me a few minutes. I can get it. I know it."

Matt used his shirt to wipe his face and head before discarding it amongst the leaves and trash. Then he jammed down on the pedals and got the crank gear spinning.

While falling into sand dunes wasn't hard, biking on the gritty earth was, and he was prepared for this. He shifted forward on the handlebars, white knuckled the rubber grips, lifted his backside off the seat, and hovered as his quads burned and did the work. With each revolution he gained more momentum. Sweat poured down his brow and past his cheek and dripped onto the machine below him. The humid air didn't quench his lungs, but it didn't matter. He was running on pure adrenaline. Ridges from the metal pedals ground into his bare feet. He stared forward, finding his zone, his happy place.

"You said you're good at fixing things?" Matt said in between breaths.

"Yes sir. Had to learn when I was a young'un. Growing up on the farm and all."

"How much longer do you think I—" he swallowed hard "—need to go?"

"I'd guess just a few minutes," Cody said. "Actually, rest now. I can feel the power radiatin' from this baby."

Matt slumped back onto the seat, fell forward, and rested his head on his sweaty forearms.

Cody turned the ignition, and the engine groaned at first, then turned over with a loud boom. Old belts whined in protest. Then the machine roared to life.

Lightbulbs lining the porch popped and exploded.

"Yes!" Cody said. "You did it, Matt!"

"I just hope it lasts longer than a few minutes," he replied.

"Oh, I'd guess you powered it up for at least an hour, maybe two. Depends how many hours this gennie has on it."

"Hey!" Catherine called from an open window. "We've got power in here. What did you do?"

CHAPTER 9

Matt and Cody rushed back into the main hall.

"Wait." Matt abruptly stopped. "What is that?"

Gears grinding and popping encompassed the air around them, but nothing in sight made the noise.

"Maybe it's the generator." Cody walked back and pressed his head on the machine. "It's running. But I don't think it's coming from this." He pounded on it with a fist. The ruckus ceased. "Huh. That's my move. Works every time."

"Good work," Matt said. "Let's get back to the group."

Matt sidestepped a broken plank and walked into the cabin. Now with the room fully illuminated, they could fully appreciate how run-down the main cabin was. Matt walked over to a poster that had fallen to the ground. He lifted the frame away from his body and dumped the broken glass onto the floor. It was of Hulk Hogan tearing his yellow T-shirt off his overly tan body. He straightened a Magic Johnson poster that hung askew on the wall and hung up Hulk Hogan next to him. The basketball court curled at the edges.

"This looks like a lot of water damage," Matt said.

The stage area sagged in the middle. Wooden folding chairs were rickety, likely termite food until the world went to pot.

"What did you do out there, chief?" Justin asked. "On the first day, Matt created light."

Rhett and Nathan laughed.

"We found a generator." Matt shimmied his skintight tank on over his sweaty body. "Its power comes from an independent bicycle. We'll have to take turns charging it. But I think it'll work for now."

"Yay." Kim twirled her hair. "Can I go swimming now?"

"Fine," Matt said. "Do whatever. How's Lance?"

"Still asleep." Catherine pointed to the stage. "We found some blankets and put him up there. He doesn't seem to be in distress, just out."

"Maybe you should kiss him, like Snow White." Stacy laughed. "Are you his Princess Charming?"

"I'll leave the making out with strangers to you, Stacy," Catherine said.

"We found an entertainment cart," Victoria interrupted. She plugged an orange extension cord into an outlet in the nearest wall. A black, metal-framed cart on wheels housed a thirty-inch tube television and both a VCR and Betamax player on the middle shelf. "Should we see what's on those tapes?"

Matt grabbed a black plastic tape marked *1* from the pile. "Kim, if you guys want to go swimming, go ahead.

Or maybe dig graves for the scientist and the girl? If not, then try to find the mess hall and find us something to eat or drink while you're at it."

"Excuse me," she said. "I'm not your maid. I won't be doing any digging. And if I stumble upon some Hi-C, then I do, but it's not because you asked me to do your bidding. Rhett, Stacy, Justin . . . and you, artsy girl, Victoria, you coming?"

"Yes." Victoria stood. "I need to get centered, if that's okay."

"You don't need my permission," Matt said.

"Whoa, whoa." Justin stood so quickly his wooden chair toppled over. "Are we just supposed to trust you to watch these videos and what, report to us?"

"Stay if you want," Matt said. "I'll be just as surprised as you to see what's on them."

"I'm gonna stay for a bit. See for myself what these mysterious tapes have to offer. Doesn't anyone else find it strange he just happened to have these tapes in *his* pod?" Justin righted his chair, then sat. "I'm not sure I trust you, chief."

Matt ignored Justin and powered the TV to life. Fuzzy black-and-white snow covered the screen. He pressed the power button on the VCR, then put Tape 1 in and pressed play. The video started for just a moment before the screen returned to snow static. The machine whined as it rewound the tape.

"Of all the times someone wasn't kind and didn't rewind," Catherine sighed.

"Speaking of kind, can you kindly wash that blood

and gore off your arms and legs?" Stacy asked. "Gross me out the door."

"Totally." Catherine crossed her arms. "You find me a shower, and I'll get right on that."

An audible click ended the tension in the room, and Matt hit the play button once more.

The scientist, albeit a couple decades younger and sans beard, sat on a simple black stool. He wore the same round Coke-bottle glasses that were now crushed into his face. His white lab coat was new and pressed to starchy perfection. Behind him, stacks of twelve-inch, gray computer monitors with green screens flickered. Many of them had graphs and charts; the others had DOS coding on them. Matt even recognized *King's Quest* on one in the corner.

"Hello," the man said. "If you're seeing this, one of three things has happened."

CHAPTER 10

The man adjusted his glasses, then said, "First scenario: the apocalypse is over, and you all survived. Congratulations. It was my pleasure to maintain the cryovault and your cryopods throughout this time. Although it is lonelier than I anticipated, you all kept me busy. Normally a mixture of cooling liquids flowed through you, keeping your cells in a near-halted growth state. But you still may have had small growth changes, like sloughing skin cells and slightly longer fingernails. To stop this process completely, I added a little cryo cocktail," he grinned, "of my own invention to each of your cryotubes. This stopped hair and fingernails from growing. Overall result: your growth process stopped entirely."

Matt rubbed his fingers over his buzz cut. *He was a brilliant scientist.*

"Dear listener," he continued, "I hope the apocalyptic weather is quick and I can be here when you awaken. I look forward to meeting you all if scenario one comes to fruition."

He cleared his throat. "The second scenario: I have grown too old or sick to continue to take care of the necessities, and I've woken up my successor, Darin. Darin, you have all the information already, and I recorded these tapes mainly for posterity. Thank you for carrying on.

"Third situation: something terrible has happened with the vault. This is highly unlikely, but I must be prepared, for all humanity rests on my shoulders.

"I will be documenting some of my day-to-days as well as giving updates every few years. I supposed I'll record a few times when I'm in need of conversation as well. Please do not judge me too harshly, and know my intentions and actions have been valiant from the beginning."

"Geez," Stacy said. "How long ago was this video taken? Looks like the guy's aged a hundred years. Cave air must be bad for your skin."

"Tha-that's rude," Nathan said. "He's been looking after u-us and keeping us alive." He stood and walked toward the door. "I'm going to dig a grave. It's the right thing to do. If anyone wants to help, meet me at the west side of the bu-building. I think I saw a shed."

"I'll help." Kyle followed him out. "Fill me in on what's on the tapes, okay?"

"Sure." Matt nodded. "Thanks for doing the heavy lifting."

They walked out, and Matt could have sworn that the seemingly mild-mannered Nathan slammed the door. Stacy was out of line, and he hoped she got the message.

"Until next time," the scientist nodded, "I bid you

adieu." He stood from his stool and walked toward the camera, and it blinked off.

Matt pressed the fast-forward button while he craned his neck toward the screen. A few moments later the black screen was filled with a close-up of the scientist.

"There's been a breach!" the frantic man yelled. An alarm droned in the background. "I'm not sure how, but something is wrong with the pods in age group seventeen." The man turned the camera around. Against a wall were pods stacked on shelves from the floor to ceiling. He panned in closer, and Matt saw his pod, number twenty. He absently rubbed the embroidered *20* on his tank top.

"See?" The man continued. "Everything looks fine, but the alarms sounded as I replenished the food. I was rummaging around, and I felt a small tremor. Maybe it was a large tremor. It's hard to tell; they've become so frequent these days that I believe I've become desensitized to them." He turned the camcorder back toward himself, inches from his face. Sweat ran down his temple onto his cheek. "I'll fix it. I know I can."

The tape stopped, and gears turned loudly inside the VCR. It clicked and automatically rewound.

"That's it?" Catherine said. "What happens next?"

"Like, that's easy. He let us out. Duh! Story over." Kim made her way to the door. "Have fun with your boring tapes. Spoiler alert, we live. Time to celebrate our 'new beginning.'"

"She's right. What else will we learn that we aren't already living?" Justin asked.

"I'd like to know where the rest of the people are.

Like my dad and mom," Matt said. "Doesn't anyone else wonder where their parents are?"

"I do," Victoria offered, meekly. "Are we all an only child?"

"No," Kim said. "I have two older brothers. All five of us were on the plane together; they must have split us up on the bus."

"Only child," Justin said. "They stopped with perfection."

"I have a sister," Rhett chimed in.

"I'm the baby," Stacy said. "I have five siblings."

"I had a brother." Cody's voice caught in a hitch. "He died when I was twelve."

"That's terrible," Catherine said. "How?"

"Texas rodeo. Got stomped on bull ridin'. Name was Wildman—the bull, that is. My brother's was Brock."

"I'm sorry, Cody," Matt said.

"You said the rest were coming, right?" Cody said. "That's why we needed to stay put?"

"I mean, I hope they are." Matt rested his arms on his knees and leaned forward. "I don't have the answers. I'm just going to keep watching the tapes and hopefully *get* some answers. If anyone else wants a break, feel free. I'll let you know what I watch."

"You do the nerd work," Rhett said. "If you come across some reruns of ALF, then I'll tap in."

Justin led Stacy, Victoria, and Kim and Rhett, who had already looped their arms around each other's waists, out the door.

Only Cody and Catherine remained.

Matt hoped he'd be able to give them some answers.

CHAPTER 11

Buzzers blared and strobe lights blinked. Chaos. The camera jiggled, then someone controlling it zoomed out and panned around the room. A dark, ridged wall came into focus. Pods stacked twenty high on shelves remained still, but a bright-red sensor blinked on each one.

"Where is that?" Matt squinted.

The camera zeroed in on the pods, then the scientist came into view. He ran from pod to pod, unplugging wires and checking tubes of fluids. Shockwaves sent the man falling to the ground. Neon-green fluid spilled onto his stained lab coat.

"It was a meteor!" the man said breathlessly. "It hit the side of the mountain and interfered with the seventeen-year-olds' pods. It took me all my courage and secret passages, but I went outside and saw for myself. I'm trying to save these kids, but I don't know if I can. I'm sorry." He pulled on the sides of his thinning hair. "I couldn't have predicted this. No one hypothesized objects from

space barreling into the earth in addition to this disas-
trous weather!"

The man disappeared behind the camera, and the screen blinked to black. Before Matt could react, it started back up.

"I think it's fixed." The scientist sat on a stool, his hair disheveled and flaking with dandruff, his cheeks flushed, eyes bloodshot. His face and hair had seemingly gone on a diet.

"What happened to this guy?" Matt whispered, leaning to the TV screen.

"The alarms go off every hour, on the hour, but I checked the vitals, and they seem correct. I'm not getting much sleep, as this has been occurring for the last week. I'm worried about the breach. The children's health is good for now, but I'm concerned that the pod system is failing. The impact to the mountain was too great. Oh, dear listener, you don't know that you're in a cave inside a mountain, do you?

"I was forced to wake my protégé, Darin. I think I may have mentioned him." A foamy crust had formed in the corners of his lips. "He tried to repair the mountain on the outside. But the weather is too harsh. He hurt his leg, and I've been helping him mend. None of this is going to plan.

"I hope I don't fail you. I'll do my best to find a way to fix the system." The room rattled. "Fantastic, another tremor. Or maybe meteor strike. Off to see what fresh hell awaits me." He exhaled loudly and walked toward the camera. "Please know, I am trying my best, and my intentions are good."

The tape clicked.

"Holy crap," Catherine said. "Are we . . . did everyone else die?"

"I doubt it," Matt said. "Only our section was failing. Wait, did you realize we were in a cave within a mountain?"

"Nope." Cody shook his head, his gray eyes wide.

"I don't even remember the plane ride." Catherine flipped her long, black curls over her shoulder.

"Do you guys remember anything from before?" Matt pressed his palms into his eyes. "I can remember things from way before getting frozen, the escort to the plane . . . then it's just blank. Completely gone. After that I remember waking up when the bus ride was over, meeting you guys briefly, then getting into my pod."

"I remember getting on the plane and being given a glass of juice," Catherine said. "They said it was for nausea and nerves. I didn't want it since I don't get sick on planes, but the stewardess wouldn't leave until I downed it. Does that ring a bell?"

"Kinda," Matt said. "Why would they drug us?"

"Yeah, wouldn't that make it harder to get us from the plane to the bus?" Cody asked. "It don't make a darn bit of sense."

"Before we start Tape 3, let's see what the others remember." Matt walked out to the covered wraparound porch, peered over the railing, and saw no one in the lake.

"Hey," Nathan yelled. "We're over he-here."

To his surprise, everyone—including Kim and Stacy—were digging two holes. Only a few had shovels; the rest used hammers, hoes, and other random items to claw at the ground.

"We'll be right there," Matt called back. He turned to Catherine and Cody. "I know you guys are skeptical. I am too. But I don't want to freak them out. Stacy has been all over the place—happy, excited, snarky, and downright mean. I think she's on the verge of cracking."

"I don't disagree." Catherine carefully made her way down the rickety porch stairs. "But I'm not going to lie."

"That's not what I'm saying. I just think we should tread lightly."

"Agreed," Cody said. "I can get behind that."

"Okay, I'm on board." Catherine fell back and let Matt lead them around the building.

Two large rectangular holes, not quite deep enough to house bodies, were formed at the edge of the camp perimeter. Someone had draped the tarp from the generator over the bodies.

"What did the second tape show?" Kyle wiped sweat from his brow with his forearm.

CHAPTER 12

"What do you guys remember about the transport here? I'm talking from the beginning to the end." Matt changed the subject.

"Why are you asking that?" Kyle asked. "The bus ride"—his face twisted in confusion—"I don't remember it. They told me I had been on one; I never questioned it."

"I remember the bus ride." Kim winked at Rhett. "It was, like, totally excellent."

Rhett wrapped his arms around her small waist and kissed the top of her head.

"Great." Matt looked to the group. "Does anyone else remember getting off the plane, or onto the bus or off the bus?"

No one spoke up.

"Okay, Rhett, Kim, spill it. Because we think we were drugged on the plane. Does everyone remember being given a glass of juice?"

"Yes," Victoria said. "It was orange juice with lots of pulp. I love pulp."

"I don't know." Kim smirked. "I guess I just saw this guy, and that's all I remember."

This is going to be like putting socks on a rooster.

Matt turned to Rhett.

"I was seated across from Kim. She kicked me, and it woke me up. She said I was stirring, and it was annoying her."

"No," Kim corrected him. "I kicked you because you were, like, talking in your sleep. It was weird. I was the only one awake. I hate pulp, so I dumped half of my juice into my mom's cup, which, I guess, explains why I woke up sooner."

"Rhett, how much do you weigh?" Cody asked.

"Two eighty-eight."

"Must have metabolized it quicker than they anticipated, or they calculated it wrong," Kyle said.

"*Anyway*, I kicked him hoping he'd tip over into the empty seat next to him and shut up. But then he looked at me with those baby blues. I was putty in his hands."

"Okay, okay." Catherine rolled her eyes. "We don't need the intimate details. What did you see outside the windows?"

"Nothing. I wasn't looking. It was dark," Kim said.

"Same," Rhett echoed.

"All I remember is when the bus was slowing down and the interior lights turned on. I think everyone else was waking up then. And we were already in the building." Matt huffed. "No one else remembers anything. Anything?"

"What are you getting at, chief?" Justin asked. "What was on that tape?"

"Yeah," Stacy echoed. "What are you hiding?"

"Nothing. I'm not hiding anything. I'm just trying to piece it together. Our cryovault and pods were in a cave inside a mountain."

"What?" Stacy yelled. "What are you talking about? No they weren't. The bus was in a warehouse, and we all exited in a *warehouse* with horrible, abusive fluorescent lighting."

"We think that building was actually the inside of a mountain," Catherine said.

"How would that even work? This is ridiculous." Stacy's voice was an entire octave higher than normal, and she waved her hands.

"That's what the tape said. And a meteor hit the side of the mountain, causing damage to the system in our pod unit." Matt held up his hands, stifling any more interruptions. "Things were bad enough that he woke his protégé, Darin."

"Do you think Lance is Darin?" Kyle asked.

"I don't know. Probably not. The scientist looks at least ten years younger than when we last saw him. Lance doesn't look that old. I'd say early twenties. We haven't seen him on tape yet because he's recovering from an injury he sustained trying to repair the damage. That's as far as we've gotten. The scientist looks haggard and tired, and he's losing hope on saving our cryopods."

"This isn't happening." Stacy burst into tears and paced in a tight circle. "Where is my mom? If I don't have my mom, who will pay my credit card bill? That means no salon." She was ranting so quickly that Matt had a hard time understanding her. "And my hair. My hair!

What man will want me without a fresh perm? How will I find a husband? I'm too pretty to be in this situation!"

"A. Husband." Victoria crossed her arms. "That's her concern."

"Hey, hey now." Justin gently grabbed Stacy by the shoulders and crouched so that he was at eye level with her. "It's all going to be okay, all right? Calm—"

"Do not tell me to calm down!" Stacy screamed.

Kim stalked over to her and pulled her into a hug and whispered something into Stacy's ear, then held her hands. "Okay?"

Stacy nodded, eyes empty and wide.

"We're going to swim, lay out, and like, relax." Kim nodded her head toward the holes. "All this manual labor and talk of—whatever it is you're implying—has gone too far. Also, the dead bodies three feet away are, like, freaking us out to the max. We're going to enjoy the next few hours. Nathan, Kyle, you got this?" She waved Justin and Rhett toward her.

"Su-sure," Nathan said.

"Yeah, you go swim, that'll solve the major problems we're facing." Kyle picked up a shovel and aggressively slammed it into the ground.

"Great." Kim smugly smiled at him, turned, and skipped toward the lake with Stacy, the two of them still hand in hand. Justin and Rhett followed.

"It's not that bad, really. Darin knows that the scientist moved us and will come looking for him—us." Matt turned to Kyle. "We'll help with the graves."

"No, it's fine," Kyle said. "Go see what's on the next

tape. And we're going to need to figure out our food situation. I didn't dare say anything in front of Miss Basket Case over there."

"I'll search for some chow. Mess hall can't be far," Cody said. "I'll meet ya back in the main cabin."

"Okay," Matt said. "You ready, Cher?"

"Very funny." Catherine brushed past him and flipped her hair. "Let's go, Sunny."

"Aren't they divorced?"

"Exactly." She tossed her head back and laughed.

CHAPTER 13

"Thanks for that." Catherine flipped on the light switch in the main hall.

"For what?" Matt said.

"The Cher thing. Made me laugh."

"I can be funny sometimes," Matt said.

"It really threw me off at first, though."

"Honestly, when I first saw you out of the pod, my brain was still so jumbled. Your hair, even matted down, looked just like Cher's to me. I guess I just blurted it out." Matt rummaged through the tapes and pull out one marked *3*.

"I took it as a compliment."

"It was."

Matt ejected the second tape, the TV hissed with white noise until the VCR swallowed the third tape. The wooden chair groaned under his weight when he sat. His hands were slick with sweat, breath pensive.

The scientist came into focus. "Good morrow! I don't believe I've formally introduced myself. My name is Dr.

Westbrook. Jim Westbrook." He rubbed his stubbly chin. His brown hair was streaked with gray, but over-all, he looked healthier. Rested. "Things are much better these days. My dear seventeen-year-olds have persevered. Strong ones. Kids are resilient. I believe the breach in the mountainside has been fixed. You see up there?"

The camera panned up to the ceiling, then zoomed in on the dark rock.

"That must be Darin running the camera," Matt suggested.

The recording focused in on thick, black foam as it snaked its away across the roof and onto the side of the cave.

"That, my dear listeners, is carbon foam. I invented it long before I was one of the only humans on earth. It was a backup, a last resort if you will. I tried all other approved options to repair the cave. Darin's youth and agility has proven invaluable. My old back doesn't bend like it used to. Darin, return the lens to me."

The camera settled into its tripod, and it focused back onto the scientist.

"The foam not only filled the cracks and holes, but because it's carbon, it actually binds to the stone and becomes rocklike. Once I began the patch work, I realized some of the steel beams had been compromised as well. No matter, carbon foam to the rescue. See?"

This time Darin zoomed out as far as the lens would allow and went from one side of the room to the oppo-site. The true expanse of the cave finally came into view—thousands of columns stacked with pods lay dormant in the cave, each section marked by a white circle and the age group painted in light blue.

"There must be five thousand pods in there," Matt said.

Catherine's mouth was agape, but she said nothing.

"How was one man monitoring that many pods? Feeding this many people? Even with two people . . . it's too much."

"I don't know," Catherine said. "If he's smart, I'm sure most of it's automated."

"Where's the power coming from?" Matt cringed. "Never mind. Solar. I forgot the government scientists found ways to save and store solar power."

"Matt," Catherine put a hand on his knee, "it's okay to question things. No one expects you to have all the answers. Okay?"

Dr. Westbrook gave the full tour of the cave. Darin remained the silent cameraman. Walls slick with humidity glistened in the artificial light. Nondescript pods filled enormous floor-to-ceiling shelves. The shelves themselves were on a wheeled track, so he could easily manipulate them if he needed more space in a particular area.

"Weary traveler, thank you for watching my videos. And remember, my intentions are good, even if I fail." Dr. Westbrook saluted the camera, and the screen blinked to static storm.

"Okay, so things seemed to have been fixed, for now," Matt said. "But why are we out?"

"How many tapes do we have left?" Catherine asked. "I need a break."

"Me too." Matt followed her out onto the balcony.

Happy screams and laughter echoed in the distance near the lake.

"They really don't have a care in the world, do they?" Matt asked. "Look at them. I don't get it."

Nathan swung from a rope swing and splashed into the water. *Guess they finished the graves.* Stacy was on Justin's shoulders, and Kim was on Rhett's. The two girls chicken wrestled, trying to knock each other into the water.

"We're all wired differently, Matt. Accept it. Yikes," she pointed to the graves, "look at those mounds. I don't think they buried them deep enough."

Two dark-red dirt mounds covered the resting places of the girl and Dr. Jim Westbrook.

"Honestly, I figured we'd need to rebury them. That's probably too close to the cabins anyway. But we'll give them a better burial later. For now, let's watch one more video, then get everyone up to speed."

Catherine rubbed her face and nodded. "Okay, *one* more."

The next tape garnered them no additional information. Westbrook continually talked about carbon foam and how he was sure it was working. That should have made Matt feel better, but the more the scientist talked, the more apparent it became that he was trying to talk himself into believing his own words.

He took them on the same tour, showing off the size of the cave, the pods, but nothing that they hadn't seen before. Finally, it ended with him talking into the camera while eating canned chili. Tomato juice dripped onto his white beard, staining it.

"As always, I bid you adieu—and know that my intentions are good."

"Why do you think he keeps saying that?" Catherine asked.

"My guess is in case he fails. He wants to be remembered as someone who did his best. Not the man responsible for killing the entire human race." Matt awkwardly laughed.

CHAPTER 14

Cody entered the room with a large army-green duffle slung over his shoulder. "Found some grub. Mostly canned stuff and MREs."

"How old is it?" Catherine asked.

"Who knows? We don't even know what year it is. But the labels are pretty faded." Cody stuffed the bag in the corner of the room. "As long as they ain't dented, or hiss when you open them, you'll probably be fine. Found these iodine tablets too. Course, we're probably better off boilin' that lake water and using the tablets together. Rhett seems like the type to pee in the water."

"Good call," Matt said. "Did you have Scout training too?"

"Nope," Cody said. "Real-life training. My daddy took us camping a lot. Made us rough it. One time he dropped me off in the middle of nowhere and told me to find home. Left me with only with a flint, backpack, and compass. He got real freaked out when the weather stuff happened. Wanted me to survive. Learn how to live off the land. He'd already lost one son; he wasn't going to lose another."

"That's pretty intense." Catherine crossed her arms.

"He was nearby, makin' sure I was fine. Taught me good stuff."

"I guess." She turned her attention toward the doors. Justin and Rhett had entered the room, dripping water everywhere.

"What did you find out, chief?" Justin asked.

"Not a ton," Matt said. "The scientist is named Dr. Jim Westbrook. He believes he fixed the breach caused by the meteor strike with carbon foam. Still doesn't explain where we are and where everyone else is."

"A meteor strike? Chyeah right!" Rhett said. "Did little green men show up too?"

"Whatever," Matt said. "You can watch later if you want."

"Is Lance still out?" Justin asked.

"Yeah," Catherine said. "I just checked on him a little bit ago. His pulse is strong, breath is even."

"Why isn't he waking from his cryosleep?" Rhett asked.

"He's just out of it, I guess." Catherine shrugged.

"Why don't you guys take a break?" Justin asked. "Come swim. It'll seriously clear your head."

"I could use a time-out," Catherine said. "Come on, Matt, please."

Matt looked back at the TV, then Catherine. "Okay," he relented. "Just for a little."

"You coming, Cody?" Rhett asked.

"Sure," Cody said. "Never cared too much for swim-min', but I could use a little sun."

Catherine made a pit stop at the shed and met them at the lake. She carefully dipped a galvanized bucket into the water and walked downhill from the lake and rinsed the scientist's blood off her arms and legs. Once clean, she ran past Matt and dove into the water.

Matt followed her in but jumped feet first instead. Cool water rushed over his body until he was completely submerged. He gently touched his belly and hurried to the surface. *I can't be in the water with an open wound.* He crawled onto a wobbly wooden dock just big enough for two people.

"Not in the mood to swim?" Catherine bobbed up and down near his legs.

"I figured it was a bad idea to bleed in our drink-ing water." He pointed to his stained tank top. "It hasn't reopened, but I don't want to take any chances."

"Or get some weird infection," Catherine said.

"Good point. Looks like they're over it too." He pointed to Stacy, Kim, and Victoria, who were lying on the soft grass next to the water. Cody, Rhett, and Justin skipped rocks. Kyle and Nathan remained in the lake. "I really do think our parents are coming."

"I do too," Catherine said. "Dr. Westbrook fixed the breach and restored our column's functionality. He wouldn't remove us for no reason. The apocalypse must be over and—wait, no." She turned pale as a ghost and pulled herself out of the water and onto the dock. "What if Darin can't leave the pods unattended?"

"He will," Matt said. "If they planned on the apocalypse outliving Dr. Westbrook, and Darin was to take over, surely there is another person next in line. Logic would state that he'd wake them, have them take over, and come looking for us."

"Sure." Catherine stood, walked along the shore toward the girls; Matt followed. "Let's see how everyone else is doing."

"How's the tan?" Justin plopped down next to Kim.

"Need baby oil." Kim rested her forearm across her eyes, shielding them from the light.

"I don't feel like I'm getting any sun," Stacy said. "It feels different than it used to. It's hot out, but it doesn't feel like the sun is what's making it warm."

"Must be the post-apocalyptic sun," Victoria said. "I never get a tan anyway."

"You're pretty pasty." Stacy laughed.

"Yeah." Kim sat up. "You're right. It does feel, like, different. This new sun totally sucks. Let's go. We're wasting our time."

"How about we split up, search the cabins. See if they're suitable to sleep in, report back to the main hall, and we'll reconvene in say, twenty minutes?"

"Whatever," Kim said. "Check for clothes too. I'd like something dry to change into. Maybe some silk pajamas if they have them."

"Wh-what if there are people in the cabins?" Nathan shuffled his feet. "Bodies. Dead people."

I should have thought of that.

"Make note of it and move on. Don't disturb the dead." Matt turned to leave before anyone else could ask questions he didn't have answers to. "And if it smells like something's rotting, don't bother going in."

CHAPTER 15

Matt watched everyone pair off and decided to crash Kim and Stacy's party of two. For one, they were the most likely to freak out (which was why he guessed that Justin and Rhett had separated themselves from them), and he wanted to calm them down before they spread fear through the entire group. And two, they were also the most likely to claim they smelled something funny and not bother checking any of the cabins.

The long path was dry. Dust kicked up with each step. Overgrown grass spilled onto parts of the path, but the quartz lining the walkways did a decent job of keeping most of it at bay. The first cabin they came upon was deeply overgrown with moss. It wicked up the sides, spreading like cancer.

"Not exactly a luxury suite," Stacy said. "We used to vacation in Aspen for every New Year's Eve. Our cabin was bitchin'. Not like this hunk of J-U-N-K."

"Aspen?" Matt kicked branches out of the alcove

leading into the entrance. "Wow. I didn't think people actually went there. Who's your mom? Goldie Hawn?"

"Ha ha." Stacy rolled her eyes.

"Holy crap." Kim placed her palms on Stacy's shoulders. "Is she?"

"No." Stacy shrugged Kim off. "My dad's a lawyer. 'Ambulance chaser' is what the guys at the country club call him. I think it's royally rude to call him that."

"So you're just, like, rich?" Kim asked.

Matt turned the handle on the front door. Their chatter was a good distraction. They seemed at ease.

"Yeah," Stacy said. "I got a Beamer for my sixteenth birthday."

"Shut up!" Kim said. "Me too! A red one! My parents are orthodontists. Or were orthodontists? Who knows now? Matt? Matt! Get out here!"

Matt waited, forcing them to come after him. The modest room held four sets of bunk beds stacked along the east and west walls. In the middle was a table with a lamp hanging from the center beam. Puzzles and board games were stacked neatly on the edge. Their colorful cardboard lids, with pictures of kids playing the games, had faded under a layer of dust. Posters of teen heartthrobs from *Tiger Beat* were tacked to the wooden walls with plastic pushpins.

"This has to be the girl's cabin," Matt said.

Along the back wall was a small kitchenette: a porcelain sink, a tiny fridge, and a hot plate on top of a chipped Formica countertop. To the right of the kitchen, a toilet, sink, and shower made up the smallest bathroom Matt had ever seen.

"Geez," Stacy said. "Talk about roughin' it."

"Let's open some windows," Matt said. "Air it out. It's a little musty."

"This is like *Little House on the Prairie* BS." Kim picked up a blanket off a bed and shook it. "Huh, I expected thirty years of dust to fall out. Not too bad, I guess."

"Can we see if there's a better cabin?" Stacy remained at the door's threshold, only poking her head inside.

"Sure," Matt said. "But don't get your hopes up. They're probably all identical."

The next three cabins were, in fact, the same. The only difference was the posters still clinging to the walls.

Matt's head started to throb.

Kim and Stacy went back to comparing stories of luxury vacations and constantly one-upping each other. He doubted any of what he'd heard was true.

"A yacht?" Matt rubbed his temples. "Who charters a yacht? Come on, even I don't believe that."

"It's true!" Stacy insisted. "It was just like that one on *Overboard*!"

"You're only saying that because I asked if you were related to Goldie Hawn." Matt cleared tumbleweeds from the entrance of the next cabin. "Give it a rest."

"Yeah, Stacy." Kim's snotty factor was off the charts. "Stop lying."

"I'm not!" Her face reddened. She rushed to the door and opened it, stepping inside first.

I guess humiliation makes her actually contribute. I'll have to remember that.

"What is this?" Stacy called out. A small thud followed.

"Is it Goldie Hawn's yacht?" Kim smirked.

Matt ignored Kim and stepped inside. A massive trunk had been tipped on its side. Musty clothes spilled out onto the brittle wooden floor.

"Nice work! Kim, get in here, Stacy found you some clothes."

"Yeah, Kim." Stacy held out a royal-blue top with yellow piping. "You owe me."

"Is that . . ." Kim froze, mouth agape.

Stacy nodded.

"Suit up, cheerleader," Matt said.

"Get out of here, perv! I need to change." Kim pushed Matt out the door before he could had a chance to leave on his own volition.

He waited outside, listening to high-pitched squeals and laughter. "Girls, can you hurry up? We need to meet up with everyone."

"Just a second," Stacy yelled. "We found it first. We get first pick."

The door clicked open, and Kim twirled. Yellow and white adorned every other pleat on her skirt.

"A cheerleading uniform! Like, can you even believe it?" Kim smoothed down the front of the loose-fitting sweater. A yellow stripe dipped across the front and continued on the sleeves. "It fits me perfectly. I feel so—so me again."

"Just don't check the zipper in the back. It's a little snug," Stacy mumbled. Stacy wore pleated, acid-washed jeans, rolled at the ankles. A short, puff-sleeved, light-pink sweater topped with a pearl necklace completed her preppy outfit. "Necklace is fake. But what do you expect? These must have been costumes for their plays. Or lost and found? I dunno, I found a few scripts at the bottom."

"Great. You guys look great and seem happy. Let's pack up and bring it to the main hall; we're late."

"You didn't see the best part," Kim said. "We have shoes! Look, they even had Kaepas."

On the sides of Kim's white cheer shoes were two small plastic triangles that matched her blue-and-gold uniform.

"They look a little big," Matt said.

"I'm not going to, like, wear ones that don't match." Kim twirled her hair. "They'll do just fine."

"Don't you want to change?" Stacy asked.

He did but thought better of it. They'd probably just take off back to the group, leaving him to carry the heavy trunk by himself. Plus, it was getting dark. An orange hue cast the entire camp in a strange glow. It wasn't like the colorful sunsets from *before*.

"Nah, let's pack it back up, and one of you can help me carry. Take turns, okay?"

"But I don't want to get anything on my sweater." Stacy pouted. "And it's the only light-pink top in the trunk. It suits my hair and skin tone."

Matt took a deep breath and shot her a stern look.

"Don't have a cow," Kim said. "Calm down. I'll take the first shift."

CHAPTER 16

"Drop it here," Matt said. "Kim, can you ask your boyfriend to bring it up?"

"No problem." She smiled. "And he's not my *boyfriend*. Not yet, anyway."

Matt climbed the rickety stairs to the main cabin, his body slick with sweat. He wasn't used to the humidity. *But it's a dry heat,* his mom would say when he complained about the desert heat.

He found the rest of the group sitting on folding chairs, oddly quiet. Victoria's porcelain face seemed paler somehow, weary.

"Great news." Matt lightly clapped his hands together to draw their attention to him. "We found a trunk of clothes. Some are pretty theater-ish, others are leftover normal clothes. And Cody found some food."

"No, he didn't," Justin said. "We got back here before him; I don't see any food. You're losing it, chief."

"He found it earlier."

"Why didn't you tell us?" Justin balled his fists by his

side. "We're starving, and you're hoarding food? I knew I shouldn't trust you."

"What gives you the right to make that decision for us?" Kyle asked.

"Whoa." Matt took a defensive step backward. "We don't have a ton at the moment, and we don't even know if it's still edible. I didn't want to pig out on what's left or get sick if it was contaminated. Plus, there are several things we need to go over before anyone starts eating. This stuff is like twenty or thirty years old."

"What's there to go over?" Rhett dropped the trunk on the floor. It bounced and dented the old wood. "I remember how to eat."

"Hang on." Catherine stood next to Matt. "You guys have been looking to him for all the answers. Then when you don't like it you give him a hard time. Either let him lead and stop giving him so much crap or—"

"Or what?" Justin took a step toward them. "Huh?"

"Or take the reins and actually do something, Justin!" Catherine squared up to him. Her long curls cascaded over her shoulders, her jaw set.

"G-guys," Nathan said, "stop fighting."

"No one is fighting," Justin said. "Trust me, if we were, you'd know."

"Is that so?" Matt puffed out his chest.

"Don't test me, *chief*. It would be over in two hits. Me hitting you, you hitting the floor."

Everyone froze.

Matt bit his lip. Nervous laughter bubbled up until he couldn't contain it for another second. He erupted into full hysterics.

"Oh, you think that's funny?" Justin gritted his teeth.

Matt held his stomach, hoping his scab on his belly button wouldn't burst open. He coughed, trying to regain his composure.

"You forgot I'm a movie buff. You stole that line from *The Breakfast Club*. Nice try." Matt laughed, then said in a mocking tone, "Me hitting you, you hitting the floor. Okay, sport-o!"

Justin's face reddened. "Where's the food."

It wasn't a question.

"Whatever, man." Matt pointed to the duffle bag in the corner. "Be my guest."

Justin stomped over to it and pulled out a can of Dinty Moore stew. "I need a can opener."

"It's at the bottom of the bag," Cody said. "But can't you wait? Matt and I have some survival training. We just need to inspect the cans and tell you what to look for, so you don't puke your guts out . . . or die."

Die.

They'd witnessed death within moments of awakening in their pods. But this was the first time anyone had talked about *them* dying. They'd survived the apocalypse and cheated death. Yet the threat of their demise lingered.

Justin twisted the silver handle on the opener; the can hissed.

"If it hisses—" Cody started.

Justin locked eyes with Cody and dumped the contents into his mouth. His eyes bulged. Cody ran over and knocked the can out of his hand. Justin doubled over, spitting out thick black goop.

"What the—are you trying to kill me?" Justin wiped

his mouth with his tank top. "Don't ever slap something out of my hand again, got it?"

"This is what I was trying to warn you about," Cody said. "If the can hisses, odds are it's contaminated with botulism."

Rhett blinked blankly.

Justin had pulled off his shirt. Rock-hard, six-pack abs flexed while he tried scraping his tongue with his shirt.

"It means it can make you sick. Sick enough to die." Matt rolled his eyes.

"I think I weeded through most of the bad ones," Cody said. "If you see one that has dents or is bulging, don't open it. Once open, if it's foamy or discolored, don't eat it. I think we should go through the canned stuff first and save the MREs."

"What's an MRE?" Victoria asked.

"Meal Ready-to-Eat," Matt said. "The military uses them. If we end up leaving, they're lighter and easier to carry." He turned to Cody. "Do you know how to make a fire?"

"Way ahead of you." Cody nodded. "I grabbed a few flints from the supply closet. Here." He handed Matt a heavy black-and-silver flint. "Justin, get in that bag and hand me a pot."

Justin reluctantly complied.

"Can someone help Cody gather some wood for a fire?"

"It's hotter than crap out there," Kim said.

"We need to boil water from the lake," Matt said. "We're all dehydrated."

"I'll help," Kyle said. "Sorry I snapped at you, Matt. This is all so confusing and stressful."

"It's fine. Anyone else who doesn't know how to start a fire and wants to learn, go with Cody."

Nathan said nothing but followed them out.

"Justin, do you want to help me divvy up the food?"

"Nope." Justin crossed his arms over his thick chest. "You said it, you're our fearless leader. You do it, chief."

CHAPTER 17

Matt sorted through cans while the others found clothes in the trunk. Faded labels of SpaghettiOs, Campbell's soups, Manwich, Dinty Moore stews, Starkist Tuna Fish, Green Giant vegetables, and Libby's fruit in sugary, sweet syrup reminded Matt of his life *before*. Cody had undersold what he'd found. He flipped over a can. Embossed on the bottom was the date *09/84*. *It would be helpful to know what year it is now.*

Matt sectioned out nine cans of chicken noodle soup and nine cans of peaches next to nine metal cups. That seemed like a decent dinner. Plus, they hadn't eaten real food in years; best not to start with something too heavy. Not only that, but Matt guessed that Justin wasn't going to try the stew again tonight.

Matt smiled and studied the rest of his group. Their clothes all seemed to match their personalities well enough. Rhett wore jorts and a red T-shirt with the number *14* heat-pressed onto it. Justin's sweatpants were high-waters, so he'd bunched them up at the knees. His hoodie looked like something a wrestler would wear before a match. Victoria smoothed her black, ankle-length, muslin dress, her pale skin a sharp contrast. *Like a modest Elvira.* The bell sleeves swished when she moved her arms. Catherine surprised Matt. He'd expected her to wear something modest and unassuming. While her white polo was nondescript, it exposed her midriff. Bright green-yellow-and-red-striped shorts grazed the tops of her thighs.

"Guess it's my turn." Matt sorted through the clothes. "Rhett, will you ride the bike on the generator for a bit, just until the others are back with the water? Catherine, can you and the others set up the chairs in front of the TV? We can eat and watch the next tape together when Cody, Nathan, and Kyle return."

"Yup." Rhett exited the room without another word.

"Sure," Stacy said.

"Great." Matt decided to press his luck since Stacy was in the helping mood. "And put a metal cup, can of soup, and fruit on each chair?"

"Kim can do that," Stacy said.

"Ugh, whatever, fine," Kim said.

Matt settled on a pair of tapered jeans, a Commodore 64 T-shirt, and a jean jacket, then changed in a nearby room. When he returned, a big pot rested on a piece of fabric on top of the wooden floor.

"The guys are back," Catherine told him. "Cody said the water is still hot, so we need to wait a few minutes. I told them to change into real clothes."

Cody was the first out.

"Nice shirt," Matt said to Cody. He wore a western

plaid shirt with pearl-snap buttons, tucked into tight jeans with a belt. "Too bad you couldn't find a belt buckle."

"Those are earned. Gotta win one. Only poseurs buy 'em."

"I wish there were an iron." Kyle tried straightening his collared shirt.

"Dude," Justin said, "you look like you're going golfing with my grandpa."

Kyle wore khaki shorts, a white Lacoste polo, and loafers. Justin wasn't wrong.

"I suppose you'd prefer I wear pajamas?" Kyle looked Justin up and down.

"NASA, gu-guys." Nathan pointed to his shirt. "I was su-supposed to go to space camp the year everything went to hell in a handbasket." He cringed. "S-sorry for cussing."

"Cute," Kim said. "Aren't you worried you're going to get those white shorts dirty?"

"They were the only ones that fit," Nathan said. "But yeah, they'll prob-probably be wrecked in an hour."

Now that everyone was dressed, Matt was slightly bummed that none of them wore a costume and they had all opted for regular clothes. Although he did agree with Kim and was happy there were boots and shoes that seemingly fit everyone.

"Let's all fill our cups, grab a chair, eat, and start the next video," Matt suggested.

"Are you sure there aren't any videos of ALF?" Rhett asked.

"Sorry, bud." Matt laughed.

Lance moaned.

Matt was first on the stage; Justin and Catherine were in tow.

"Hey, are you okay?" Matt crouched on the floor next to Lance.

He groaned, then rolled to his side.

"What's wrong with him?" Justin asked.

"I don't know. It seems like he was trying to wake up," Matt said. "Let's get something under his head for support."

Cody tossed Justin a balled-up sweatshirt from the trunk. Catherine pulled the blanket off Lance and fluffed it.

"Wait," Catherine said. "Let's take off that belt. I'm sure it's uncomfortable."

"Good idea," Matt said. He reached for the buckle. "I can't. Look. There's a small padlock on it."

"What?" Justin pushed Matt out of the way. "Why?"

No one spoke. Matt felt a shiver down his back. He covered Lance and returned to the circle of chairs by the TV and sat silently.

"Well, this is awkward," Stacy said.

"Why don't you tell us what's on the menu, chief?" Justin asked.

"This is condensed soup, but we're fresh out of bowls at the moment. If you want, you can mix it in your cup with some water." Matt held the can opener. "Or just eat it straight from the can. I think it tastes better that way anyway. Remember what Cody said: if the can hisses when you open it, or if it's foamy, discolored, or smells rancid, then toss it."

"Like I said, I think I weeded out most of the cans with rusted-out bottoms and the ones that were bulging or had dents. But double-check them anyway, okay?" Cody said. "Actually, maybe I should go around and open everyone's can and show them what to look for this first time?"

"I'd appreciate that," Kyle said. "I don't plan on eating canned food forever, but the information is good to have."

Matt handed Cody the can opener and prepped the fifth tape for viewing. Before he pushed play, he paused. "Let me catch everyone up."

CHAPTER 18

Matt paced. "We all saw the first tape together, so I won't bore you with that. At some point there was a breach. Dr. Westbrook, the scientist, didn't know what had happened. He thought it was a malfunction of the system but quickly realized that something bad had happened. Alarms went off in our section every hour on the hour. He unfroze his successor, Darin, and had him help. Remember how terrible and crazy the weather was before we were saved?"

"Yeah," Cody said. "There was an F-5 tornado in the middle of a blizzard in Texas. It didn't make no sense."

"New York had completely flooded," Victoria said. "Even if I could get back to Manhattan, it wouldn't matter. Last I saw, the ocean had swallowed the entire city. Only the tops of a few skyscrapers poked through the water."

"And remember how the temperatures would shift throughout the day? You'd wake up and it'd be one-hundred degrees, then by noon it'd be negative twenty, and by late afternoon it was seventy. All the plants died." Catherine rubbed her left shoulder. "The air got thick; it was terrifying."

"I just remember when the roof on the mall blew off," Stacy said. "We had to take cover in a tornado shelter for two days. My Beamer had blown away . . . It was horrible. A police officer escorted me home. My parents were pissed."

"Exactly," Matt said. "So when the whole mountain shook, Dr. Westbrook thought it was an earthquake. But when he couldn't find any cracks in the ground, he started looking up. It wasn't an earthquake; it was a meteor. It struck the side of the mountain, and the cave had a crack in it."

"What?" Nathan said. "Sp-space?"

"No way," Kyle said. "That's too much. The solar system is waging war against us too?"

"I think it was just a coincidence with incredibly terrible timing," Catherine said. "Go on, Matt."

"Right, okay, then Jim—Dr. Westbrook, tried repairing it, but nothing worked. He had developed something called carbon foam and used it to fill in the holes and repair everything, even steel beams. Darin did most of the actual repairs since he was younger and more agile. The thing is this—and maybe some of you knew this already—but when they showed the repairs, we saw how large the cave was."

"What are you getting at, chief?" Justin asked.

"There were thousands of pods. *Thousands!*"

"You didn't tell me that." Justin spat his words.

"I am now." Matt said. "It all makes sense. You'd

need that many people to start a new population. But it was unnerving to see. One man—well, two now—taking care of that many people."

"I wonder if we're the only cave people are stored in?" Victoria asked.

"Shut up!" Kim said. "That's, like, more than my brain can handle right now."

"She's probably right. We might not be the only seventeen-year-olds in our column. I vaguely remember there being more of us. We might have been the first ones out, then the truck—well, you know. But who knows? Hopefully we'll get that, and more questions, answered either from the tapes or Lance when he wakes up." Matt turned to Cody. "Everyone's soup okay?"

"I think so," Cody said. "Only had to replace one."

"Tastes weird," Rhett said. "But not disgusting."

"Great." Matt pressed play, sat in his chair, and smelled his soup.

Mom used to make me this when I was sick.

He stirred it with a metal spoon. It felt thick, gelatinous at first, but once it was mixed it wasn't too bad. He gingerly took a sip; a slimy noodle fell back into the can. The salty broth tasted familiar but was overshadowed by a metal tang. It wasn't great, but it would do. He downed his water, not realizing how thirsty he was until his cup was drained. *I'll save the peaches for after the video.*

Dr. Westbrook sat on a stool in his usual spot, in front of the bank of computer monitors. He'd aged at least a decade, Matt guessed. His hair had completely grayed. His face was hollow and thin, though he seemed in good spirits.

"Everything has been stable, but the apocalypse is still ongoing." He sighed. "Darin, show them the feed."

The camera zoomed in on a computer monitor behind the scientist. Grainy black-and-white footage showed feet of snow along with a lightning strike. Moments later, a comet zoomed across the sky, blinding them for a moment. Then the camera shook.

"Holy suck!" Rhett yelled.

"Ah." Dr. Westbrook smiled. "Another meteor strike. They're becoming more frequent these days. I can't deduce what it means without additional information. Maybe things are getting worse, irreparable. Or not. I can't say, unfortunately."

A row of monitors blinked out behind him. A voice off camera alerted him.

"I bid you adieu, but remember, my intentions are good." Dr. Westbrook stood and walked slowly and carefully toward the monitors, slightly hunched and shuffling his feet. It reminded Matt of how his grandpa walked. The scientist pulled cables and cords out of the monitors just before the footage ended.

"Wow," Stacy said. "These tapes are boring. I think I'd just like your CliffsNotes version in the future."

"He's really gotten old," Nathan said. "H-h-how long were we frozen?"

Matt's head spun. "Hang on, this doesn't make any sense. The apocalypse was still happening when this was filmed. And Dr. Westbrook didn't look much older after the crash than he did in the video."

"So what?" Justin said.

"So, how are the trees so big? How has this entire

place regrown? Those redwoods are at least a few hundred years old. No way that much time has passed."

"Maybe the entire world wasn't hit with the erratic weather." Justin shoved a syrupy peach into his mouth.

"I doubt that," Matt said.

"But you don't know, do you?" Justin asked. "How could you know? You got eyes and ears everywhere? No. Obviously this area wasn't hit too hard, and nothing was destroyed. How else do you explain the cabins and stuff, chief? Huh?"

Matt chewed on his bottom lip. "New York City is now part of the ocean, and you think this place was untouched?"

"Look around." Justin stood and splayed his arms out. "Unless we're all tripping on mushrooms, then yes."

"What do you think?" Kyle turned to Catherine. "You saw all the other tapes."

"Justin's right, this place does seem untouched. But logic, and what Dr. Westbrook has said . . . it doesn't make any sense."

The room fell silent.

CHAPTER 19

"It's getting late. I think we should sleep on it and have clearer heads tomorrow." Matt rested his elbows on his knees and hung his head. His chair squeaked.

"Gotta find a way to prove you're right, don't you?" Justin asked. "Fine, take all night. But you can't deny what's around you."

"Justin, I'm not the enemy. Yes, this is all here, you're right. I'm just having a hard time connecting the dots, okay? This all seems strange to me. The only logical thing is that the apocalypse is over, and he was moving us here to live. We were moved first because our column was the most in danger. I'm sure Darin will be bringing others soon. From the cryovault . . . from the cave."

"I'm scared," Stacy said.

For once, Matt thought she was being genuine. "I don't want to split up."

"Me either," Kim said.

"M-maybe we should all sl-sleep in here tonight?" Nathan asked. "Together?"

"Safety in numbers—good idea." Cody stood and clapped his hands together. "I think I saw some sleepin' bags in one of the backrooms."

"I saw them too," Kyle said. "I'll help."

"Great," Matt said.

They set up their sleeping bags in a circle, heads toward the middle. Once the sun had set, it was pitch-black outside. Matt stared out the window. No stars, no moon. Justin insisted that it was just cloudy; Matt silently disagreed. A green lantern in the center of the group illuminated the room. Awkward conversation only lasted a few minutes before it was lights-out.

Matt felt the tension. He knew he wasn't the only one questioning things. But he understood why people sided with Justin. Instead of sorting it out now, Matt closed his eyes and drifted into his first natural sleep in a few decades.

The hard floor beneath Matt vibrated. His eyes flashed open. "Does anyone else feel that?"

Before anyone could answer, gears popped loudly.

"I think it's the gennie," Cody said. "Like what we heard before."

"This loud? In here?" Matt asked.

The grinding grew louder, and the entire room shook. Metal screeched and groaned.

Victoria screamed.

"What the—" Matt stood. Then everything stopped. "That was weird."

"Wh-what w-w-was th-th-that?" Nathan's voice trembled.

The grinding and popping started again, but this time the room remained still.

"I'm going to turn off the generator." Matt lit the lantern. "See if that helps."

"I'm coming too," Justin said.

"You guys aren't leaving us." Kim stood, put a blanket over her shoulders like a shawl. "No way. That's like, literally the start of every horror movie, Voorhees."

"Yeah, I'm coming too." Stacy mirrored Kim and wrapped herself in a flannel sheet.

"Okay," Matt said. "Let's all go."

"Not me." Rhett turned on his side, eyes sealed shut. "Too tired."

"Rhett, get up!" Kim kicked his legs.

He groaned but didn't move.

"Fine," Kim said. "Then I'll find someone else to keep me safe."

"Okay, okay." Rhett stood, wiped the sleep from his eyes.

Matt led the group down the stairs, the lantern his only source of light. No crickets, grasshoppers, or cicadas buzzed, just the sounds of their footsteps on the dirt ground. Fog curled around their ankles. The heavy air felt thick in his lungs. Around the corner, the yellow beast hummed.

"I'll turn 'er off." Cody switched the key to off, and the whole unit shuttered to a stop.

"That's it?" Victoria asked. "Just like a car?"

"Yup," Cody said. "But always leave the key in the ignition. These suckers are easy to lose."

Matt held his hands out like he was surfing. "Whoa!"

The grinding shook the ground below their feet.

"I thought you turned it off," Rhett said. "What the hell?"

"He did," Matt said.

"I guess it had a bit of stored energy still in it?" Cody's voice cracked on his last word.

"An earthquake?" Kyle suggested. "Maybe the apocalypse isn't over."

"Dude, we already talked about this." Justin ran his hair through his messy blond hair. "Look around, it's over. We've had normal weather all day. What else could it be? I'm going back to bed."

Justin took the lantern from Matt and started back toward the cabin. Matt wrestled with what to do, but ultimately followed the group. It was too early in the morning to have a real conversation. The hairs on the back of Matt's neck stood erect. The generator had been turned off, but the noise and tremors still happened. It didn't make any sense. He said nothing on his way back to the cabin and kept his head down. *If I panic, they panic.*

Kim clicked on the light switch. "Ugh, can we turn the generator back on? It totally freaks me out not having power. Like, what if something happens?"

"We just shut it off." Justin crawled into his sleeping bag. "We'll deal with it in the morning."

"No," Kim protested. "Seriously, like, I can't deal with this. I'm going to have a panic attack."

"Does anyone else mind if we have it on?" Matt settled into his sleeping bag.

"No," Kyle said. "Let's have it on in case of an emergency. If the ground rattles again, we know it's just the generator. Nothing to worry about."

"All right," Cody said. "Nathan, you wanna grab the lantern and I'll show you how to turn it on?"

"Su-sure." The tall, thin boy held the lantern and walked side-by-side with Cody as they exited the room.

The silence was deafening. Now with the room completely devoid of light, Matt shivered. No matter how much he told himself things were fine, he couldn't shake the ominous feeling. He wrapped his arms around his legs and waited for his friends to return.

CHAPTER 20

"I'm wired," Catherine said. "I don't think I'll sleep anymore tonight. What time is it?"

"I dunno," Matt said. "The sky is barely purple, maybe four?"

The door creaked open. Nathan nodded in Matt's direction.

"Gennie's on," Cody said.

Stacy quietly cried in her sleeping bag.

"It's okay." Catherine rubbed Stacy's back. "We're going to be fine."

"I'm so scared," Stacy said. "That sounded purposeful. Like someone is after us."

"You watch too many movies," Justin said.

"Speaking of movies. How about you put on another episode of Jim Westbrook: boring-est and only man alive? That'll put us to sleep," Kim said.

Matt felt her sarcasm but took the opportunity to watch the sixth tape. He crossed the room and pushed the black plastic cassette into the VCR, hoping for an answer.

With the lantern off, the TV cast a flickering white light on the room until the video started.

"Greetings, gentle listener." Dr. Westbrook sat on a stool in front of a stack of pods. "I'd like to show you a bit of what I do up close. See this?" He moved to the side and held a thin, clear tube connected to a pod. Green lights lit up at the base, one by one, toward the top. "See how quickly they move? This is a good feeding tube. Connections are strong, delivery is consistent and effective. Not like this one." He pointed to the one above it, then disappeared from the frame. The camera shifted up toward it, then zoomed in. "See how sluggish the lights are, indicating the flow? And the last two don't light up. The tube is getting clogged with crud and must be replaced."

Dr. Westbrook came back into view and climbed a small ladder with a clear, plastic replacement in his teeth. He pushed a button on the side of the pod, and it hissed and steamed. The tube fell free from the top, and he worked quickly, securing the new. Blue lights lit up.

"I've got six different colors of lights to use. Currently green are the oldest and blue are the newest. I haven't had to dip into the other four reserves yet. You see, I must check 5,253 apparatuses every single day. This helps me move quicker, although I still must check the newer ones in case they are defective."

He disappeared behind the camera, and the lens moved toward the base of the shelf. Once back in view, Dr. Westbrook pulled a thick foam piece from a trap door on the galvanized frame. When he held it up to the camera, Matt recognized it as an air filter. Black dust covered it.

"We recycle the air, but it gets old and stale. This acid kills the dust, and the oils stimulate serotonin when inhaled."

He used an ordinary spray bottle, like the one Matt's mom used to keep the cat off the countertop, and sprayed the filter. Neon-yellow specks dotted it; one more spray and it was coated. The concoction looked alive. It rolled and zoomed around the surface. A yellow ball formed and twisted with black gunk. Finally, it rolled around the entire surface and fell off like an old piece of Silly Putty detaching itself from the ceiling. The filter was clean as new.

"Whoa," Matt said.

"This task isn't as hard, since one filter services eight to ten people. Admittedly, it's my favorite. There's something deeply gratifying about cleanliness." He picked up the ball of gunk and tossed it into a wastebasket.

The scientist was now behind the camera. "Now, this chore is my saddest one." The camera was set on the ground, and the tripod came into view. The camcorder moved unsteadily, then was seemingly placed securely in the cradle. He stood in view again with a flashlight. "I'm checking the door for cracks. The air quality is beyond hazardous at times, and I don't want it, or the erratic temperatures, leaking in. You see, this job saddens me because this was Darin's favorite task. I'm sorry to inform you, dear listener, that Darin has perished."

Matt's heart sank.

"Went mad, really. As the young people used to say, he had a freak-out. Couldn't take the isolation or pressure of the job. He exited the cave and is presumed dead. You see, he left during a lava flow wrought with acidic rain activity. It was one hundred fifty-eight degrees out-side. Not only did he leave in horrible, impossible con-ditions, but he did it in his underwear. Marched to his death, really."

Matt felt the words form on his lips but didn't recog-nize his own voice. "Darin is dead."

"Dear Darin, how I miss you. I often wonder, if I had known your internal struggles, would I have unfrozen you? Could I have done this without you? And that is the reason why I won't awake anyone else unless I am near death. I wasted a life. Please forgive me. My intentions were good, and yet Darin has died."

Click.

The light from the TV now cast gray tones across the room. Loud snow on the screen. Matt swallowed hard, unmoving.

CHAPTER 21

Matt stood and slowly paced the room. He'd never even seen Darin, yet he couldn't get the image of a deranged man, clad only in his underwear, clawing at the door, desperate for an escape. *Is that what I'm doing?* He knew he had to choose his words carefully.

"I think we should go." Matt took a deep breath. "Darin is dead. There's no one left to get us. We need to find the cave and figure out how to maintain or unfreeze everyone."

"Okay, chief, let me get this straight. You were the one who insisted we stay, now you want us to go?" Justin snickered. "Sounds like you're losing your marbles. I never believed in you to begin with. Now I trust you less."

"Justin, stop," Catherine said. "Matt was right to have us stay. How could he have known Darin was dead?"

"He couldn't." An orange glow from the sunrise cast a menacing glow across Justin's face. "Just like he can't know if the scientist woke someone else up later."

"True," Matt said. "I don't. But he said he'd only do it in an extreme case."

"Like death?" Stacy said. "Because that happened."

"But he didn't know," Matt said. "He died in an accident. He wasn't sick."

"How do you know!" Justin's voice boomed. "That's right, you don't. How about this: you leave, I'll stay."

"I'm not trying to split us up. I just want to make sure our parents and brothers and sisters aren't unattended in a cave somewhere, dying. Don't you care?"

"I don't have a savior complex, chief. What I do have is a roof over my head, food, water, a few hot babes to flirt with, and best of all, a righteous lake. So while you're busy trying to fix a world that isn't broken, I'm going to take care of me."

"What a prince," Catherine said under her breath.

"Maybe we should have some breakfast?" Victoria said. "I think we might be a little hungry."

"Go ahead." Matt took the can opener and unsealed his peaches from last night. "I'm going to pack up some stuff and walk to the truck, see if it's salvageable. If it is, I'm following its tracks and driving back to wherever it came from."

"Good riddance," Justin spat.

"I'm coming," Kyle said. "The hostility in here is uncalled for. And I'd like to make a decision based on evidence I see with my own eyes."

Cody rummaged through the duffle bag and picked out a few supplies and deposited them into two green canvas backpacks. "You guys go ahead. I'm going to turn off the generator. I don't want anyone messing with it if the noises return."

"Anyone else?" Catherine asked. "Once, twice, no? Then it's settled, Matt, Cody, Kyle, and me."

"Nathan, will you check on Lance throughout the day? Make sure he's breathing," Matt said.

Nathan parted his lips but said nothing. Instead he simply nodded.

"Wait," Victoria said. "I'm not a good hiker, and I can't fix anything. I won't be any help . . . but you guys are coming back, right?"

"Yes," Matt said. "We'll be gone all day—overnight at the latest. If it's farther than that, we'll come back for you guys with the truck. But we'll be back, we won't abandon anyone. Not even you, Justin."

"Whatever, chief. You're burning daylight."

Matt stormed out of the cabin. His emotions had gotten the better of him, and he slammed the door shut behind him.

"I don't claim to have the answers. I have the same information you all have. I'm just looking at things logically. *Logically!*" Matt kicked a rock; it bounced into the tall grass. "Dr. Westbrook is dead. Darin is dead. The other girl from our cryopod column is dead. There could be others stuck dying in their pods. We still don't even know why he was moving our cryopods. We can't sit idly by and hope another successor was awakened before Dr. Westbrook was crushed."

"My daddy used to say, 'Hold out two hands, shit in one and hope in the other, tell me which one fills up first.' I know it's crass, but he ain't wrong, and neither are you." Cody said. "Gennie's off."

"Matt, you're not doing anything wrong." Catherine jogged beside him.

"We need to find our parents," Kyle said. "Maybe I should have stayed behind and watched the next tapes, maybe get some more answers."

"If you want to go back, then I understand." Matt stopped and faced Kyle. "But ever since I realized the vault could be unattended, all I can think about is my parents suffocating. And if not that, then severe dehydration is likely starting to set in."

"I think it was all automated," Kyle said. "Isn't it?"

"We think, but as Justin pointed out, we don't *actually* know. We only know what he showed us." Matt walked under the *New Beginnings* arch into the forest. "You saw all the checks Dr. Westbrook did every single day. I have to err on the side of caution. My conscience won't let me assume everything is okay. The entire human population could be on the line."

"Don't worry about that," Cody said. "I'm pretty sure Kim and Rhett are already workin' on repopulating the earth."

Matt laughed. He stopped and grabbed his stomach. Frustrated tears streamed down his face while he laughed.

"First of all, that's disgusting," Catherine said. "Secondly, we needed that. Thank you, Cody."

Matt wiped his eyes.

"You don't have the entire world on your shoulders." Catherine faced Matt. "I know it feels that way, but you're doing your best. We all are."

"Even Justin," Kyle said. "He's a dick, but he's just as clueless as the rest of us. You know? Some people just handle it better than others."

"You're right," Matt said. "Looks like the sun is fully up. I guess we better hurry. *We're burning daylight.*"

CHAPTER 22

"Did you guys notice the lake?" Kyle asked. "It was higher this morning."

"Now that you mention it, yeah. I thought it looked fuller," Catherine said. "Like it might crest the banks."

"How?" Cody asked.

"Maybe it rained last night?" Kyle said. "It would explain the fog."

"But the ground wasn't muddy. Not even damp," Matt said. "Are you sure it was higher?"

"Either that or the rope swing got longer," Kyle said. "It's almost touching the water."

Matt looked at the snowcapped mountain in the distance, through the massive trees.

Curious.

Another mystery he had no way of solving. Not yet anyway. His shirt clung to his body. He removed his jacket and hung it on a branch close to the path. *I'll pick it up on the way back.*

"Kyle, you said you were from Connecticut?" Catherine asked.

"Born and raised."

"You don't have an accent," she said. "Not even a hint."

"You'll hear it in my *o*'s on occasion, but not anywhere else. My mom was a WASP; I wasn't allowed to have one."

"Honestly, I thought you were snobby at first," Catherine said.

"I get that a lot," he said.

"What did you do up in New England for fun?" Matt asked.

"Normal stuff. I was class president every year of high school. Raised enough money for both a prom and a class trip. First class to ever do that. Took the entire class to the Hamptons for a day of ice skating."

"Oddly specific, but sounds fun," Matt said.

"You'd have to count me out," Cody said. "I'd never seen ice or snow until the apocalypse. Wouldn't know how to skate if I tried."

"Not true." Kyle proudly puffed out his chest. "We had coaches on site for the unfortunate ones who didn't know how. Everyone had a wonderful time."

"I bet you play tennis in the summer too," Catherine said.

"Of course I did. I wasn't meant to be the next Andre Agassi, but it was fun, nonetheless. Great for networking."

"You're a funny guy, Kyle." Cody patted his back. "We grew up very differently."

"And it's a good thing we did," Kyle said. "Our diversity is what keeps the group moving forward. So many different skills in a small group. It's a true melting pot. Just like our founding fathers intended."

Matt stifled a laugh; the kid was more intense than he'd realized. It was nice getting to know him outside the influence of Justin.

"Does anyone remember how much farther the truck is?" Kyle asked.

"I don't think it's far." Matt wiped sweat from his brow. "Has anyone else ever changed a tire before?"

"I have," Cody said. "Lots. Trucks, cars, farm equipment. Even a golf cart once. That sucker was harder than I expected."

"I have too," Catherine said. "My dad made me learn when I got my license. Then I'm pretty sure he sabotaged my tire to hammer in the point; I got a flat soon after. But I changed it and ruined a perfectly good sweater in the process."

"Great. That's awesome." Matt shifted his canvas bag on his shoulder. "Not about your shirt, though. Sorry."

Catherine shrugged.

"This will be an excellent opportunity for me to learn and stay out of the way. But I'll pay close attention." Kyle frowned. "I wish I had brought something to take notes."

"I don't think we'll be changing many cars' tires in the future," Matt said. "Unless there is a fleet of solar-powered vehicles."

They laughed, then walked in silence. For a minute, it felt like they were roaming the halls on the first day of school and they were all the new kid. Backpacks on their shoulders, awkward, forced conversation that quickly led to commonalities and friendships. It felt normal. Like *before.*

Matt's calves burned as he hiked up the last hill. He recognized the area. Red dirt stained his white shoes. As he crested the top, he saw the truck; it sat cockeyed. And behind it, a puddle of dried blood. Dr. Westbrook's final offering lay baking in the sun. He stared at it while he caught his breath.

"I wonder how different this would all have been if he'd lived. If he hadn't blown a tire. If he hadn't been crushed." Matt said.

"I know, buddy." Cody rested his hand on Matt's shoulder. "But all we can do is be thankful he got me out before it happened, or else . . ."

Matt fell silent. Cody was right.

"Let's get to work, then eat after?" Matt asked.

"Sure," Kyle said. "But I'm starving."

"With this many people, it ain't gonna take long," Cody said. "It'll be done lickety-split."

"Guys, I don't see a spare," Catherine said.

CHAPTER 23

"Crap." Matt's hands shook with nervous energy. "I didn't even consider that."

Matt checked the back of the truck. Nothing. He closed his eyes and took a deep breath. Searched his brain. His eyes flipped open. "It's underneath. I've seen this before, in a movie."

The truck sat cockeyed on its front passenger side where the tire had blown. Looking under the cargo area revealed a large, full-sized tire and jack wedged against the fuel tank. All of the parts under the truck had a white *B-35* painted on them.

"I'll help." Cody slid underneath on his belly, then flipped onto his back. "I wonder what that means?" Cody asked, pointing to a number.

"I dunno." Matt loosened the jack, and it landed on the pine-needle-covered ground next to him.

"Cody"—Matt lay next to him, wedging his fingers under the tire—"when we first met, you mentioned a meltdown. Dr. Westbrook said something about the truck and the meltdown. What did he mean?"

Cody froze. "Gosh, I guess I forgot he said that. Let me think."

Matt chewed on the side of his lip. *How could I have forgotten about that?*

"I—I guess he didn't really say much. Just that the truck had wrecked, and he needed me to help him get the pods open. There was an emergency. He said something, like maybe he was having a meltdown, I think."

"Are you sure?"

"Geez, I just don't remember. It was so hectic." Cody jostled the prongs, and the tire came loose.

Matt grabbed the side of it when it broke free; Cody had the other side.

"Kyle, Catherine, take this." Matt shoved it toward them, then grabbed the heavy rusted jack. "It's okay, Cody. I get it. It was crazy. I forgot about the conversation until we were back here. If you remember anything, let me know."

Matt shimmied out from under the vehicle and paused. The air felt different, still heavy and hot, but almost electric. Gooseflesh broke out over his skin. He still hadn't seen the sun. It was a disorienting feeling. Catherine had rolled the spare and propped it against the bumper. Matt concentrated on his conversation with Cody, hoping to trigger something. Maybe he'd heard him wrong, but it felt like there was something there. He handed Cody the jack.

The steel frame moaned as the jack lifted it to the proper height. While the rubber had ripped free, the lug nuts remained on the wheel. Cody worked quickly, unscrewing them.

"Did you feel that?" Kyle asked. "The ground, did it just move?"

"No," Catherine said. "Stop being paranoid, you're gonna freak me out."

The last lug nut fell and hit the ground.

Pop!

Gears ground and metal groaned, echoing through the forest. Matt whipped around.

"What *is* that?" Catherine asked.

Matt's blood turned to ice. He shook his head. "This is impossible. We're nowhere near camp."

A crack of thunder boomed, and a streak of silver lightning ripped across the darkening sky. Thick, puffy clouds formed out of nowhere, colliding. Rain poured from the pluming clouds.

"Hurry," Catherine said. She rolled the tire to Matt.

Matt pushed it on, his hand slipping in the wetness.

Cody walked to the edge of the hill.

The lug nuts became slick, but Matt shoved them on one by one.

"Water!" Cody ran toward them. "It's a flash flood."

"What?" Kyle yelled over the rain. "Impossible."

"It's coming!" Cody reached for the passenger door. "Get in!"

Matt stripped the final lug nut and wiped his brow. A fruitless effort in the downpour.

Matt jumped onto the driver's seat. Catherine, Kyle, and Cody piled onto the front bench seat. With shaky hands, he twisted the ignition; the engine hummed and clicked. He turned it again, this time pumping the gas. "Come on." It sputtered and turned over. "Yes!"

Water had already flooded the road. His dad had always told him to never drive into water. Flash floods were common in Nevada. But nothing like this. *Sorry, Dad.*

Matt backed the truck up a few feet. Water lapped at his ankles. The vehicle lurched forward. Creeping forward, he felt the tires sink. He floored it, but the truck was no match. The force of the flowing water slammed the truck into the trees.

"There's too much," Cody said. "We're stuck."

"Get on the roof," Matt said.

"We'll get swept away," Kyle said.

"What do you suggest?" Matt forced the door open and climbed from the sidestep to the hood, then onto the roof. "Come on." Matt reached for Catherine's hand and pulled her onto the hood.

Cody met Matt on the roof from the opposite side and pulled up Kyle, who immediately lay flat on the roof.

"Stand up!" Catherine yelled.

"No!" Kyle lay flat on his stomach. "This is safer."

The ground below them became a raging river in a matter of seconds. Logs and forest debris roared past. It was like white-water rafting on the Colorado River. A tree trunk smashed through the windshield, rocking the heavy vehicle.

"We need to get in a tree!" Matt jumped up and slipped, landing on his left wrist. Pain shot up to his elbow.

Cody planted his feet and slowly stood. He held onto

a nearby limb and held his hand out. Matt reached up on unsteady feet.

"Go!" Matt yelled.

Cody climbed onto a thick branch, then up one more, and sat.

Matt grabbed Catherine's hand and boosted her into the tree. Heat radiated through his wrist.

"Can you climb up to Cody?"

She nodded.

The truck lurched again. Matt held on for dear life.

"Kyle!"

Kyle still lay flat on his stomach, holding the edge of the interior roof.

"Come on, you have to get up!"

"Just—just give me a second." Kyle's voice trembled.

Water rose rapidly.

Matt climbed fully onto the branch. He extended his arm down toward Kyle.

Kyle released his grip on the headliner and reached up.

Matt grasped Kyle's hand. "I got you."

Rain beat down even harder. Kyle's slippery hand squeezed Matt's so hard it was hard for Matt to hold it back. He pulled, his shoulder felt like it was coming out of his socket. Catherine or Cody had yelled something at him, but he couldn't make it out over the roar of the flood.

"Don't let go!" Kyle screamed.

"You have to get up!" Matt shouted. "I can't pull you into the tree."

Kyle tried to stand and lost his footing, pulling Matt

with him. Matt squeezed his thighs around the branch. Bark cut into his legs. Matt felt a hand on his shoulder.

"Matt, stop!" Cody yelled into his ear. "He's gonna pull you into the water."

"Get up!" Matt yelled at Kyle, ignoring Cody. "Hurry! The water's rising!"

Kyle grasped Matt's hand.

A clap of thunder cracked so loudly Matt's teeth vibrated.

Matt turned his head, looking up the tree at Cody. "Pull!" Both of his shoulders were pulled in opposite directions. He screamed.

The newly-formed river raged harder than ever. A huge downed tree smashed into the side of the truck.

Pure horror was etched on Kyle's face. He thrust back as if someone had jerked him from behind. His grip on Matt was severed. Eyes wide with shock, he bounced off the roof of the truck and splashed into the water.

"No!" Matt screamed. "Kyle!"

CHAPTER 24

A wave rushed over Matt's entire body. He wrapped his arms around the branch and felt it fracture.

"Kyle!" He desperately scanned the area.

The limb sagged dangerously low, but Matt didn't care. He dangled his arm in the water, feeling for his friend. Sharp, jagged debris crashed into his soft skin.

"Come on, Matt!" Cody tugged on him a final time. "Get up here."

The branch cracked, and he relented. Matt followed Cody up onto the closest branch, then onto another one near Catherine. His wrist protested, but adrenaline pushed him through.

"Can you see Kyle?" Matt yelled over the raging river.

The truck tumbled under the water. A tire surfaced as the truck rolled, then slammed into two trees, wedging itself between them.

"No," Catherine cried. "The log, I saw it hit the truck. Kyle—he just—he just fell into the water. I haven't seen him surface."

"Maybe he grabbed onto a tree," Cody said. "He can swim."

Matt leaned forward, resting his head against the trunk of the tree. The rough bark dug into his forehead. His chest heaved as he caught his breath.

The rain quit as suddenly as it had started. Clouds parted, and the sky was bright again. The river swirled and receded. Like someone had pulled the plug on a bathtub.

"This is so weird," Catherine said. "I know it's the new normal, but it isn't normal to me at all."

"I don't get it either," Cody said.

"As soon the river is at tire height, let's climb down. We have to find Kyle," Matt said.

He scaled the tree when Catherine stopped him.

"Is it safe? Should we wait in case it rains again?"

"Kyle could be hurt. This is my fault." Matt jumped into waist-deep water. "Kyle!" he yelled.

Cody and Catherine soon followed and spread out. The water had completely receded, and Matt's feet stuck in the mud like a suction cup with each step.

"Anything?" Catherine called out.

"Nope," Cody said.

"No," Matt whispered to himself as he pulled a piece of material off a fern. He held the alligator logo from Kyle's polo. "Guys, over here."

Matt stared at the ripped hunk of shirt, willing Kyle to be okay. He held it out for them to see.

Catherine opened her mouth to speak but said nothing. Instead, she searched the area and called out his name.

Matt parted thick bushes, hoping his worst fear wouldn't be confirmed. Then he saw a shoe sticking out of scrub brush.

"Kyle?" He gingerly touched the shoe, hoping it was empty.

It felt hard.

Then he saw the other foot. He grabbed hold of both legs and immediately dropped them. Cold. Kyle was cold to the touch. *Maybe it's just from the water.*

A voice he didn't recognize yelled for Catherine and Cody. His vocal cords strained as he called out again.

Everything felt like it was in slow motion. He watched Cody pull Kyle from the foliage. Kyle's shirt had ripped free of his body. Blood seeped out of dozens of cuts on his chest and bruised ribs. His arm bent in an unnatural way; his skin was purple. Worst of all was his face: frozen, horrified, and wide-eyed. Catherine ran to his side and crouched next to him.

"Hey, hey, are you okay?" Catherine shouted. She tilted his head back and parted his lips, then gasped. "No, no, no."

Matt stared in disbelief. She shoved her fingers into his mouth and produced a fistful of wet leaves. Then she placed her left hand over her right, interlaced her fingers, and straightened her elbows.

Chest compressions.

She counted to fifteen, then pinched his nose and breathed into his mouth.

"Come on." Catherine pressed on his chest again. Sweat dripped down her temple. Again, she filled his lungs with air. "Kyle, wake up! Wake up!"

"He's gone." Matt put his hands over hers. "There's nothing we can do."

Catherine leaned into Matt's chest and sobbed. He wrapped his arms around her and stroked her long, black curls, streaking them with his muddy hands.

"Catherine, I'm sorry. You have to get up. We need to get back to camp."

"Camp." She jumped to her feet. "Crap! I forgot about them. I was so—so. I'm sorry."

"Don't be." Matt turned to Cody. "Are you okay?"

Cody's pallor wasn't much better than Kyle's. He turned and retched. Acidic bile and last night's dinner wafted in the humid air.

"Sorry 'bout that." Cody nodded, as if he were tipping his cowboy hat at them. "Seen a lot of dead livestock in my day, but nothing like this. What do we do, Matt? Bury him or leave?"

"Let's carry him to the truck and come back for him after we check on the others. We'll bury him after we check on everyone else." He cringed. "I know that sounds bad, but we don't have a choice right now."

"Okay," Cody said.

Matt held Kyle's wrists, and Cody held his ankles. They shimmied over to the truck, which was now wedged between two trees. The windshield had been obliterated. A tree poked out of the grill. Radiator fluid leaked, staining the wet ground.

Kyle's lifeless body lay next to the truck. Matt closed Kyle's eyes, like he'd seen in so many films. But his eyelids popped open. This wasn't the movies.

They walked in silence for a few minutes. Puddles

from the leftover flash flood dotted the landscape along with trees and ripped branches. Parts of the path were nearly impassable with the debris.

"Dang it," Cody said. "That flood washed away the truck's track marks."

Matt rubbed his face. "I didn't even think of that. This sucks."

The ground rumbled under his feet. His heartbeat quickened. Then he heard the dreaded pop and grind.

CHAPTER 25

"Get in a tree!" Matt screamed. He laced his fingers together to create a step. Catherine's shoes dug into his palms, and he boosted her up. Pain again shot through his wrist. "Cody, you're next."

Cody waved him off and took a running start toward a thick redwood. He jumped and caught the branch, swinging until he had enough momentum to pull himself up.

Matt tried the same but missed. He found purchase on the side of the tree as the ground rumbled again. Popping and grinding. As if the earth was awakening.

"Climb higher!" Matt shook his left wrist and grimaced.

Camp!

He climbed up until branches were too far away or unstable, then leaned out as far as he could. No clouds in sight; Matt shielded his eyes from the bright light.

Then he saw it.

It wasn't the camp they'd left.

A newly formed lake encompassed the entire valley. Chimneys from a few cabins poked through the water. The only building exposed was the top half of the main hall.

"Are you guys seeing this?" Matt asked.

"Yes," Catherine said. "The flood, it happened so fast. I hope . . ."

Matt sat on his branch for a few minutes, still searching for signs of life and monitoring the sky for weather.

"How long should we wait up here?" Catherine asked.

"I guess we can get down now?" Matt guessed. "It just seems like every time we hear the noise something terrible happens."

"It didn't last night," Cody said. "But I'd rather be safe than sorry."

"Me too," Matt said. "But I guess something should have happened by now. Careful when you climb down."

Pain radiated through his left arm. Matt ignored it. Kyle was dead; no one wanted to hear about a sprained wrist. He waited for his friends to dismount the tree before he brought up the next topic.

They walked for a few minutes toward camp. Catherine silently cried. Cody's eyes were wide, blank, and expressionless. This wasn't a good time to bring it up, but he had no choice.

"I feel the closest to you two." Matt took a deep breath. "And I hope you guys feel like you can trust me."

"Sure, buddy," Cody said, putting his arm around Matt's shoulders.

"I don't want to freak anyone out, but—"

"The apocalypse." Catherine interrupted him. "It's not over, is it?"

Matt bit his lip. "Maybe not. But maybe so."

"Why would he unfreeze us?" Catherine asked. "It doesn't make any sense."

"It had to have something to do with the initial breach, right?" Matt asked.

"We gotta get back and watch the tapes," Cody said. "Hopefully he has the answers there."

"I doubt it. If he was as panicked as you said he was, I'd be shocked if he took time to record a message." Matt misjudged the depth of a puddle and post-holed up to his knee in mud. "That's the other thing. Camp is flooded. We don't know if anyone else is hurt, or . . . or like Kyle. And the tapes! I hope they didn't get ruined."

"Crap on a cracker," Cody said. "Maybe we can dry them out."

"It won't matter if the TV got fried." Catherine kicked a rock. "Ugh, how is this happening? Why did Dr. Westbrook do this to us? We came so far, and now he just leaves us here to—what? Die one by one?"

"He didn't mean to leave us," Matt said. "Catherine, he was crushed. I'm not saying the apocalypse isn't over, but I'm also not saying it is. That might have just been a random flash flood."

Matt hoped she believed him. He wanted to believe himself. But deep down, he knew something was very, very wrong.

"Have you noticed that?" Cody took a deep breath. "It's not fresh. I used to love the smell of rain. The plants ain't blooming; the birds ain't chirpin'."

Matt inhaled the heavy air and smelled nothing. He rubbed a hand over his prickly hair and stared at the ground. His head swirled.

The ground quickly became a slippery, muddy mess on their final descent down the hill. At the bottom, a couple feet of water still remained. Matt slogged through it, wishing he'd opted for shorts. Water wicked up his pants. He paused at the *New Beginnings* sign.

"No matter what, we stay together, and we stay calm. Okay?" Matt managed to keep his face expressionless, but a muscle ticked in his jaw.

"Roger that," Cody said.

Catherine nodded. "So much for our new beginning."

CHAPTER 26

The flood in the camp hadn't fully receded like it had elsewhere. But it made sense, since it was in the valley. Debris from the cabins floated in the knee-high water. When they'd first jumped into the raging river to find Kyle, they'd only encountered organic material. But here, old clothes, waterlogged folders and papers, along with mattresses, sheets, and pillows, floated in the newly formed lake that was Camp New Beginnings.

They waded through it, tripping every few feet on unseen trees and rocks below. Matt's foot caught something hard, and he fell, arms out to catch himself. His left wrist buckled immediately upon impact, leaving his right arm to take the brunt of the fall. Murkiness clouded his vision. He felt someone pull the back of his shirt and lift him out of the water.

"Thanks," Matt coughed.

"You're weak," Catherine said. "We need to eat."

"We will." Matt trudged carefully through the muck.

"Is that . . ." Cody squinted.

"Rhett!" Matt called.

The large boy paddled a small yellow canoe through the water. The front end sagged. It would be a matter of minutes before it would be rendered useless. Water swirled and rapidly retreated, draining into a low spot between the main cabin and the lake.

Matt high-stepped it toward him.

"Hey! You guys made it back," Rhett yelled. He stood and exited the watercraft.

"We're so happy to see you," Catherine said. "The others, are they . . ."

"They're in the cabin." Rhett yanked off his shirt, wrung it out, then slipped it back on with a shiver.

"What happened?" Matt asked.

"We were swimming, and all of a sudden it started to rain big time bad. Kim," he rolled his eyes, "got all freaked out because she thought she saw some lightning. Then Stacy joined in. Total hysterics. They demanded we take cover inside. I mean, have you ever met anyone that's been electrocuted?"

Matt furrowed his brow. *Big dumb animal, isn't that what Kyle whispered? He had him pegged.*

"So we walked toward the hall just to shut them up, and the lake leaked into the camp."

"Leaked?" Catherine folded her arms. "You mean, it crested its banks? Major flash flood?"

Rhett smiled—big straight, white teeth. As if he was posing for a team photo.

"Rhett, it was serious." Catherine continued, "We were stuck in trees and saw that the entire camp was underwater. All the cabins, sheds—everything except part of the main structure.”

“That was the thing. The girls were already up the stairs. We got caught in it the last few steps and swam up to join them in the cabin. Where’s Kyle?”

“The cabin didn’t flood?” Matt ignored his question. He only wanted to recount that story once.

“Oh yeah, follow me.” Rhett waved them toward him. “It flooded a bunch. Past the deck and into the gym. Probably two or three feet high.”

“But everyone is okay?” Catherine asked. “You all made it to safety.”

“Yep.” Rhett walked up the first few steps and out of the water. “Even the sleeping guy is okay.”

Catherine turned to Matt. “How is he so casual about all of this? He has no idea how bad this could have been and *was* for us.”

Matt’s spine stiffened. “Do you think the lake flooded before? Maybe that’s why the floors inside are so warped? Same with the railings and porch?”

“Maybe.” Cody turned white as a ghost. “That means it’ll happen again.”

Matt shrugged and trudged up the stairs, his mind reeling. The swollen door caught on the deck when he forced it open. Inside, Kim, Stacy, and Victoria huddled in a corner, faces tearstained. Justin lay on the stage; Nathan sat on the ground below him. A waterline on the exposed logs was two feet high.

The door scraped loudly when he released it. All eyes were on them.

"You made it back, chief." Justin sat, dangled his legs off the stage. "Where's my ride?"

"We got caught in the flood," Matt said. "The truck is wrecked."

"Way to go." Justin slowly clapped. "Not another car on the street, and you still managed to total our only vehicle."

"Shut up, Justin," Catherine said. "You have no idea what we've been through."

"Yeah, you look pretty rough," he said. "You been rolling in the mud or what?"

"We got there and changed the tire; it was sunny skies. Then . . ." Matt rubbed his face. "I don't know. Suddenly it was raining, bad—like how it would rain right before we were frozen in the cryovault. Without warning, there was a flash flood. We got in the truck, drove a few feet, and within seconds there was water in the cab. The river smashed the truck against a tree. We got out onto the roof—"

"No way," Nathan said. "Th-th-the lake was up to the tr-truck."

"Doubt it," Cody said. "I reckon it was just a flash flood. Coincidence."

Matt stared at the floor. It was still damp, the wood curled worse than before. "It all happened so fast. We climbed onto the trees, and Kyle . . ." Matt's shoulders slumped. "He was still on the truck. He was swept away by a wave."

"What?" Victoria jumped to her feet and ran to the door. "We have to go find him."

Matt stopped her and held both of her shoulders. "We found him. Kyle is dead."

CHAPTER 27

"Get out," Stacy said.

"I'm sorry," Matt said.

Everyone approached him; he held his ground.

"What do you me-mean dead?" Nathan asked, his eyes filled with tears.

"He drowned." Matt took a small step backward.

"This is your fault." Justin balled his fists. "It was your idea to go to the stupid truck in the first place. Now look, you have no truck and Kyle's blood is on your hands."

"That's not fair," Catherine said. "Kyle panicked. He wouldn't let go of the truck and climb onto the tree."

"He wouldn't have been there if it weren't for you three," Rhett said.

"And what if we had stayed here?" Cody stood next to Matt. "There's no sayin' where he would have been or if he would have made it back to the cabin in time. Least we were out looking for a solution."

"Where is he?" Victoria's voice was barely above a whisper. "His body."

Catherine took Victoria's hands into her own. "He's still there. We saw camp was underwater and ran here first to see if you guys needed help. We'll go back and get him. Bury him like we did with Dr. Westbrook and the girl. Okay?"

"I hope you jerks do a better job burying Kyle than you did the scientist and the girl," Justin said. "We saw a body float by about twenty minutes ago."

"So-sorry." Nathan hung his head. "You gu-guys left us to swim. Kyle and I did our best."

"Now Kyle gets to join them, thanks to Matt," Justin said.

Victoria sobbed quietly.

"Now what, *chief*?"

"That's enough!" Catherine shouted.

"The tapes, where are they? Are the TV and VCR okay, or did they get wet?" Matt asked.

"Can you, like, shut up about the stupid tapes already?" Kim screamed. "You act like they're going to give you a secret code to this crap. Like, enough already!"

"Yeah," Stacy said. "All you've done is boss us around, coddle the tapes, and get Kyle killed."

That stung.

"Hey, that ain't fair," Cody said. "If it were up to you, all you would have done is swim and frolic in the sun. He directed us to find food, clothes, and shelter. Isn't that somethin'?"

"Not worth a life," Stacy muttered.

"Here's the 411: none of us are safe." Matt's face

flushed. "Justin could have died when he ate the rancid stew. Heck, you could step on a nail and die of tetanus. There are things we can avoid, like drinking tainted water or injuring ourselves. What we can't avoid are natural disasters. I'm done fighting. Where are the tapes?"

"Whatever." Kim turned on her heel and walked away.

"Bottom of the TV cart." Justin smirked. "But I don't think you're going to be happy."

The cart had been shoved in the corner near the stage. Matt stalked over to it. He patted the TV and VCR. Both felt dry to the touch. At the bottom were all nine tapes. Water pooled at the bottom of the tray.

Matt cursed.

"We gotta get these dried out, see if they still work." He picked them up. Water leaked out of the holes.

"Dude, take a chill pill," Stacy said. "It's not like we have anything else to do."

"Nathan, did you see any screwdrivers in the shed?" Matt ignored her.

"Ye-yes," he replied. "What kind?"

"Phillips. Bring a few. The screws are pretty small." He turned to Cody and Catherine "Help me bring these outside?"

"Sure." Cody grabbed four tapes.

"I'm going to stay here, try and explain this again to them, okay?" Catherine whispered to Matt. "You're not the enemy."

Matt nodded, rummaged around the backroom for a towel, took the remaining tapes, and left.

The waterlogged wood stairs felt soft under his feet.

Like they were made of foam. It was only a matter of time before the supports rotted out and the wraparound porch collapsed. That was a problem for another day.

"That rain really cooled it down." Cody shivered. "Wind picked up too."

"Yeah, it did." Matt yelled toward the shed, "Nathan, we're on the east side of the cabin."

"Won't they dry faster in the sun?" Cody asked.

"I don't think the tape can be in direct sunlight. I mean, that's how camera film works. Well, they can't see light at all. But these are like cassettes. I think they'll fare better in the shade. Hopefully they're not completely soaked and the breeze helps dry them out."

Nathan met them with six screwdrivers. One had a grease-stained handle that was still neon orange on the very top and bottom. It said *Trav's Auto Care 555-2744* on the side grip. The other five were clear plastic, standard green.

Matt reached for the colorful-handled one first. "Hope this works."

On top of the faded *Gremlins* beach towel, all nine tapes lay ten inches apart. Matt carefully unscrewed one side of the tape, and the other. He wedged his fingers in the small space and evenly applied pressure, careful not to break the plastic.

Pop!

He placed the casing directly below the tape, laid the screws in it, then examined the innards as if he were doing an autopsy.

"Okay, see?" Matt pointed to the reels. "This was completely rewound. That was in our favor. The roll is tight; it looks like only the first few layers got wet. And they might still be playable. Cody, you start on that end, Nathan the middle. If it is partially unwound, let me know and we'll decide what to do. If you're feeling nervous, open one of the tapes we've already seen first. We cannot break Tapes 7 through 9."

Matt removed four more black plastic covers and discovered the same thing: all had been completely unwound or rewound.

"You guys doing okay?" Matt asked.

"I cracked the back piece on Tape 3," Cody said. "But if we need to rewatch it, we can swap it out with one that's intact."

"That's okay," Matt said. "Nathan?"

"A-all good."

"I think this is the best spot for them to dry. If we hear any popping or grinding, our first priority is to meet here, grab the towel, and bring it inside and up high. Hopefully that's a nonissue today. For sure, we'll bring them in at night."

"Works for me," Cody said. "What about the generator?"

CHAPTER 28

"Crap," Matt said. "I guess let's see if it starts. Nathan, do you want to help or see if you can find some smaller pieces of wood that have dried out already? We need to get a fire going."

"Sure," he said. "I'll see if any-anyone else wants to help."

Matt rounded the side of the building with Cody in tow. Broken trees, mattresses, and bedding from cabins had crashed into the side of the generator.

Stale, wet mildew wafted from the soaked mattresses. *This isn't the first time it's flooded. Who cleaned up last time?* He pulled one off the machine and dropped it onto the ground. Cody dragged a heavy branch from the back end of it.

"I dunno," Cody said. "I ain't ever tried to start one after a flood."

"Should we wait? Will it damage it?"

"Might. But I have an inkling this one is different, considering the modifications from the bicycle."

Matt pressed his hand against the side with his good hand. No humming. His heart sank.

"I hope it's not ruined." Matt kicked the side. Water trickled out of one of the seams. "I guess we can wait until tomorrow. Let's help with the fire in the meantime. At least get our bedding dry before night."

Matt stared at the clear blue sky. Afternoon had faded into a deep blue, as if the sky was preparing itself for the sunset. He and Cody grabbed branches and broken limbs on their way back to the front of the cabin. Nathan waved at them and pointed to his small pile of wood.

Two logs of similar size had been speared into the ground, six feet apart from each other. Stacy stood on one side of the makeshift clothesline with a rope near the top of the log. Kim mirrored her on the opposite side.

"Ready," Stacy said.

Catherine pressed a nail through the coarse rope and pounded it in, then did the same on Kim's side.

"Great idea, ladies." Matt turned to Nathan. "Any of the wood dry enough to burn?"

"Ki-kinda," Nathan said. "Justin is looking for dry paper to use as kindling." He continued to break small twigs and stack them in a cone.

"Can't believe he's actually helpin'," Cody said.

"He said he wa-wants a dry blanket." Nathan rolled his eyes.

Victoria traipsed down the long staircase, arms overflowing with matted sleeping bags.

"Here," Matt met her halfway up the stairs, "let me help."

The sleeping bags were considerably heavier than

they had been before. He draped one over the clothesline. The line sagged in the middle at first but righted itself once more bags had been evenly spaced over it.

"This is great. Can you make a few more like this?" Matt asked Kim and Stacy.

"I guess," Kim said.

"I'll help." Victoria touched a post. "These shouldn't be too hard to find. How many more should we build?"

"Three or four, I reckon." Cody yelled toward the cabin. "Rhett, Justin, get down here."

"What?" Justin yelled from the balcony.

"You find some paper?"

"Yeah," he said. "We'll be right down. Keep your shorts on."

Matt and Cody placed the bigger logs near the fire pit while they waited for Justin.

"All we could find were old playbills from the cabinets in the dressing rooms by the stage," Justin said.

"That'll work." Matt tore the black-and-yellow magazines into long strips and placed them between sticks. "We'll have to rotate these logs and branches near the fire. Get them dry."

"The bags are too far away," Rhett protested.

"An-any closer and they'll melt," Nathan said.

Rhett shrugged.

Matt pressed his hands near his pocket and felt the outline of his flint. He pulled it from his pocket, thankful it hadn't been lost in the chaos. He struck the metal across it; a small spark jumped from the end. One more strike and a tiny fire erupted.

"Hand me a few sticks," Matt said. He gently blew

on the fire then placed a few thicker sticks near it. "That's right. Burn baby, burn."

The girls returned and built four more clotheslines. Rhett used an old, rusted ax to break them into smaller logs.

"It's getting dark," Catherine said. "I'm going to grab us some dinner. I haven't eaten yet today."

"Me neither." Nathan followed her up the stairs. "Sh-should we check on Lance too?"

"Good idea," Matt said. "If he doesn't wake up soon . . ."

Catherine nodded.

The remaining teenagers sat in a circle around the fire. Shadows danced across their faces as the sky faded from orange to black. Rhett held Kim as she sobbed quietly. Justin tried to comfort Stacy, but she rebuffed his advances. The breeze from the afternoon had turned into a gusty wind. Matt wrapped his arms around himself, wishing he still had his jacket.

And Kyle.

CHAPTER 29

They all ate metallic-tasting stew except for Justin. He opted for SpaghettiOs and complained there wasn't any Tang to chase it down. Cody had boiled water for everyone, then boiled a second batch to be stored in the cabin.

Cutting the wood had helped it dry out considerably faster. The fire roared; Matt held his hands out, catching the warmth.

"Guess we should bring the tapes in before we turn in," Matt said. "Just in case."

"Ugh!" Kim yelled. "Can you, like, shove it with those tapes? I wasn't kidding before. I've had it with your heinous ideas. Come on, Rhett. Let's take a walk."

She stood, holding Rhett's hand, and pulled him up from a log. He waved goodbye but said nothing. Within a few seconds, they disappeared into the darkness. A few minutes later, Matt heard the distant opening and closing of a cabin door.

"N-n-no stars or moon again tonight," Nathan said, craning his neck toward the night sky.

"Hmm, the sleeping bags aren't quite dry yet, but mostly." Catherine flipped them one by one until each one's damp side faced the fire.

"It's okay. We can hang out a little longer." Justin winked at Catherine.

I guess he's moved on from Stacy to Catherine.

"I'll be back," Matt said, in his best Terminator voice. "Cody? Nathan? Will you bring a lantern with you?"

"You're breaking my heart, chief." Justin put an arm around both Catherine and Stacy's shoulders. "You leaving me out?"

"Nope." Matt balled his fists at his sides. "Just leaving you to tend to the fire."

"I'll keep 'em warm." Justin smirked.

Matt's nostrils flared, but he thought better of saying anything and walked away. He led Nathan and Cody to the east side of the main hall. Nathan held the light while Matt held one end of the towel and Cody held the other. They carried their precious cargo and walked slowly, careful not to lose any screws or disturb the open reels. As the stairs had dried out, the wood had curled more fiercely and made it even more precarious to climb.

"Careful," Matt said.

"I ain't one to complain," Cody said, "but this porch has seen better days."

Nathan opened the door and illuminated the dark hall. "Now where?" he asked.

"Um, how about one of the tables up on the stage by Lance?" Matt replied.

Nathan again led the way, and they placed the towel

on the stage. Matt jumped up first, and Cody followed. He froze.

"Wh-what?" Nathan asked.

"Hang on." Matt jumped down and placed his hand on the ground as if it were train tracks and he was feeling for an oncoming train. "Nothing. I thought I heard something."

"You did," Cody said. "I heard it too, but it wasn't as loud this time."

"Maybe it's nothing," Matt said.

"Wh-what do you mean?" Nathan asked.

Matt made eye contact with Cody.

Cody nodded.

"We heard those popping and grinding noises out by the truck, right before the rain and flash flood. It might be related." He quickly returned to the stage and helped Cody place the towel and all the VHS tapes onto a rickety card table. "But we heard it again later and nothing happened. Okay, these tapes should be good."

"How'd they look?" Nathan asked.

"They're still pretty wet," Matt said.

The front door slammed open.

"Hey," Catherine said. "Get out here!"

"What?" Matt jumped down and jogged toward Catherine.

"It's snowing."

Matt shook his head. "No. No way."

Loud footfalls echoed up the stairs.

"Believe it, chief," Justin said. He held several sleeping bags. "Guess I'm not getting my own room tonight."

Victoria and Stacy followed behind him with the rest of the bags. Matt slammed the door shut.

"We've got to find Kim and Rhett." Stacy shivered.

"Forget them," Justin said. "They know where we are."

"I agree with Justin," Matt said. "We need to move the dry wood into the shed. The fire should burn out on its own. We should only go in and out if it's absolutely necessary; we've got to save the heat in here. Lighting the fireplace should be a last resort. We have no idea the last time it was serviced or if the flue is blocked. Anyone who wants to help with the wood, follow me."

Everyone followed. Victoria held the lantern. Ice-cold wind whipped the snow around their feet. Luckily it was only flurries. They had to keep the firewood dry.

"Ow," Stacy said. "This bark is sharp."

"Suck it up, buttercup," Justin said.

"Kim," Stacy yelled. Her voice cut through the wind. "Kim!"

Catherine and Victoria joined in.

Matt trudged back and forth with Victoria leading the way. Wind bit at his exposed skin and seeped through his shirt. He tucked his head down. Finally, most of the wood had been safely tucked into the shed. He looked in the direction of where Rhett and Kim had run off to. Smoke snaked its way from a chimney in a nearby cabin.

"Look," he yelled over the wind.

"I can't believe that Rhett figured out how to make a fire," Catherine said. "And what are they burning?"

"Who cares," Matt said, and he ran toward the main hall.

He raced up the stairs and waited until everyone was behind him before he opened the door, then quickly slammed it once they were all tucked inside.

"Holy crap," Cody said. "It's like Alaska out there."

"I don't think the apocalypse is over," Catherine said.

Matt bit his lip. "I don't know. It—nothing makes any sense."

"I found a few candles in the stage area yesterday," Victoria said. "Can you use your flint to light them?"

"I think I can handle that," Cody said. "Good find."

Three red candles jutted up in a tarnished silver candelabra. Once lit, Victoria extinguished the kerosene lantern. An eerie crimson glow filled the room.

Stacy walked to the window. "Why is it so damn dark? I hope Rhett and Kim are okay."

"It's just a little snow," Justin said, putting a hand on her shoulder. "It's barely even accumulated. It's just the wind that sucks. I'm sure they're keeping warm in a cabin, if you know what I mean."

"Gag me with a spoon," Stacy said. "I'm going to bed."

"Good idea," Matt said.

They placed their sleeping bags in a small circle again, this time short three people. One by one they fell asleep. Catherine rested her head on Matt's shoulder.

"I'm scared," she whispered.

"Me too." Matt wrapped his arm around her and fell asleep.

CHAPTER 30

Matt slowly blinked sleep out of his eyes. The candles had burned down, leaving a waxy puddle under the candelabra. Bright light shone in from the windows, the kind that only sun reflecting off fresh snow produced. He gently shook Catherine, waking her.

"Hm?" She held the back of her neck and sat.

Matt shimmied out of his sleeping bag and approached a window. Three feet of fresh powder covered the ground. Trees white with frost. His breath fogged up the glass. Lazy wisps of smoke from Kim and Rhett's cabin rose in the cold air.

"I wonder how long they're planning on staying there?" Matt tapped on the glass in their direction.

Bang! Bang! Bang!

"What the—"

"Is that Kim?" Stacy bolted toward the door.

Matt stepped in front of her. His hands trembled as he palmed the knob.

"Or Rhett?" Stacy's voice cracked.

It wasn't.

"It's not coming from the door." Catherine slowly approached the stage. "It's Lance."

The tall man rolled on his side, scratching his throat and pounding the stage with a closed fist.

"Water," Matt said. "Get him some water!"

Cody dipped a metal cup into the saved water and presented it to Lance, who greedily drank it down.

"Are you okay?" Matt stood in front of his group, an arm's length away from Lance.

"I think—" His voice caught in a coughing fit.

"Move," Justin said to Matt. He reached for the cup and left to refill it. He returned and handed it to Lance. "There you go, drink it down."

The man's hands shook, and he only sipped the water this time.

"I feel so weak," he said. "Where am I? How long was I out?"

"We'll get you some food," Matt said. "You've been unconscious for as long as we've known you, so almost three days now. We're at a camp called New Beginnings."

"What's your name?" Cody handed him a can of Manwich and a spoon.

"Thank you." He focused on his meal and ate. Orange stained the sides of his lips. "Where did you get this?"

"Found it in the mess hall," Cody said.

"Thanks—" He froze. "Where's Westbrook?" He threw his blanket off and pawed at the Everlast weight-lifting belt.

"He's—he's dead." Matt held his hands up defensively.

"Dead?" Lance's eyes grew wide.

"Calm down. It's going to be okay. He was crushed by a pod—"

"The key, where's the key!" he shouted.

"What key?" Justin asked. "Are you looney or what?"

"The one that opened the pods. I need it."

Catherine pulled a silver chain tucked into her blouse from her neck. "This?"

"Please." He held out his palm. "I'll die without it, and so will you."

"Who *are* you?" Matt spat.

"I'm Darin."

CHAPTER 31

"No way," Matt felt the color drain from his face. "The protégé? No, he died."

"Died? I didn't die. What are you talking about?"

"Yes, that's what Dr. Westbrook said in his video. You went crazy and died." Catherine palmed the key.

"So you are cuckoo for Cocoa Puffs," Justin said. "Great."

"What?" Darin shook his head. His feathered hair swished. "No, I'll explain everything—just give me the damn key."

"After you explain," Matt said.

"This belt is an explosive device, and I have no idea what detonates it. Let me take it off so we're safe. Okay?" Darin's tone had softened, and his words were even.

Catherine didn't hand him the key but instead unlocked the padlock on his belt, then placed it back around her neck. "Good thing I saved it."

"Yes." Darin exhaled loudly and removed the belt.

"Is it safe to go outside? We need to get it out of here. As
far away as possible."

"Yeah, it's fine right now. And you're not leaving,"
Matt said.

"I'll take it." Victoria gingerly picked it up. "Is the
forest okay?"

"No," Darin said. "Too much potential shrapnel. Are
there any barren spots in camp?"

"May-maybe the back of camp, opposite of the
entrance?" Nathan suggested.

"Yes," Matt said. "Good idea."

Nathan jumped off the stage and reached up to Victoria to take the belt. "Let's go."

"I can do it," Victoria said.

"What if it starts to snow again?" Nathan asked.
"P-p-pairs are better."

Matt nodded, and they left. A cold gust of wind bit
through the air when they opened the door.

"Snow?" Darin asked.

"Don't change the subject," Justin said.

"How are you not dead? And you're not old enough
to be Darin from the video. If he had lived, he'd be like
thirty or forty." Matt sat on the stage floor and stared at
Darin.

"Let me explain. I was in the twelve-year-old column
when I was frozen. One day Westbrook woke me up. I
had no idea what was going on. He said I was to take
over for him if the apocalypse outlived him. He seemed
perfectly healthy, but I worked with him day in and out
for years. Maybe ten or so? I'm not sure. He was—odd,
to say the very least. As young as I was, I still felt like

something was off about him. He called me defiant and ordered me back into my pod, said I wasn't ready, that I had disappointed him. The last thing he said before he put me in the cryopod again was, 'Darin, you are dead to me.'"

"That doesn't explain why you're here now," Matt said.

"Why *am* I here? Where is here?" Darin stood on wobbly legs. "You said there was snow. How bad?" He stepped down and approached a window.

"Pretty bad. We got like three feet," Catherine said. "It came out of nowhere. We're worried the apocalypse isn't over. Look, we need to find our families."

Matt put a hand on her shoulder. "And we want to know why Dr. Westbrook woke us up if it wasn't safe."

"This isn't bad," Darin said. "Snowstorms aren't unusual. Look, you can see the sky. The air isn't hurting my lungs. It's worse in some spots. On our way here, it was just as bad as before. This must be some sanctuary. I wonder how he found this place?"

"I've had it!" Stacy yelled. "Tell us right now what's going on or—or I'm going to kill you. You got it?"

"Calm down, Stacy." Matt turned to Darin. "We aren't going to kill you. That's insane."

"Westbrook was insane." Darin stared at the ground.

The room fell silent.

"He woke me up—I guess three days ago. He was manic, frenzied," Darin continued. "Fifteen years must have gone by; he looked so much older. He didn't give me a second to acclimate. The moment I stood, he put the belt around my waist and told me to help or else. The alarm was buzzing so loud, warning strobe lights blinking reds and greens. It was chaos. I refused to help until I knew what was going on. Then he told me that the column that I—he told me that the column that had broken when I was first awake was failing. That the seventeen-year-olds were dying. We needed to move them and wake them up. I asked why the weight belt. I'd use a forklift to move the pods. He said it was a bomb—insurance, really, so I'd be forced to help. If I didn't, he'd detonate the device and kill me and anyone within a hundred feet."

"Why didn't he trust you to help?" Matt asked. "We were dying."

"I didn't fully trust him when he put me back to sleep. I was the only one awake, and where could I go? Out into the apocalypse? Let's just leave it at that. Anyway, he'd backed the emergency truck into the cave, and I moved as many pods as I could fit into the cargo area. Once it was full I jumped into the cab. No idea how we were going to unload the pods or where we were going. I honestly assumed we were just going to a different area of the cave." He stared blankly out the window at the snow. "But he drove to a big set of doors, made me open the right side. I was afraid he was going to lock me out. As soon as I opened the door I was hit with intense heat. The air was so thick and polluted. In the few seconds it took for him to pull the truck out and me to shut the door and get back in the truck, I was coughing up black mucus. The sky was an orangish-red. Wind swirled. Tornados everywhere. Lightning strikes shook the truck; I was worried about the pods. It was terrifying. We were on a death drive. Once I caught my breath, I tried to ask

Westbrook where he was taking us. Out of nowhere, I felt a sharp pain in my thigh. A huge needle was plunged into my leg, and the next thing I knew, I was here. See?"

Darin pointed to a round bruise on his upper thigh.

"This doesn't make any sense. Dr. Westbrook was trying to save us. Maybe he tranq'd you to calm you down. Are you sure you weren't the hyped-up one?" Matt paced. "He was good. He sacrificed his life for us."

"I knew a very different Westbrook," Darin said.

"What about the tapes?" Catherine asked.

"Oh, right! I forgot he used to document us. Wait, how do you know about them?" Darin's face twisted in confusion.

"I assume he put them in my pod," Matt said. "I guess to explain what happened, just in case. We've only watched six of the nine."

"You have power? And a TV?"

"Yep," Justin said. "We have it all."

"I need to see them. What did he tell you?"

"Does it matter?" Matt asked. "You were there."

"You don't get it." Darin raised his voice. "Whatever Westbrook told you was a work of fiction. His reality and actual reality weren't linear."

"No," Matt said. "No way. He was genuine and sincere. He looked over us for years all alone."

"You're right," Darin said. "But I was there. I saw him; he changed. The isolation unlocked something deep in him. Something—wrong. I want to see those tapes."

"Can't." Justin said. "They got wet during the flood yesterday."

"It flooded before the snow?" Darin scratched the bruised injection site on his leg.

"Yes," Cody said.

A rush of cold air filled the room, and Victoria and Nathan slammed the door behind them.

"Okay, it's done." Nathan wrapped a blanket around Victoria and himself.

"Kim and Rhett aren't out of their cabin yet," Victoria said. "I guess they'll join us when they're good and ready."

"Fine with me," Stacy said. "Kim was getting on my nerves."

"There are more of you?" Darin asked. "How many?"

"We gotta get back to the vault," Matt said.

"How?" Justin asked. "You got any snowshoes or a map?"

"No, I've got something better." Matt turned to Darin. "Do you remember the way?"

"I don't," he said. "I lost consciousness maybe fifty feet from the front doors of the cave. Besides, you guys, the air is *breathable* here. We must be really far—like hundreds if not thousands of miles from the cave. None of this looks toxic or volatile. How did Westbrook know about this place?"

"But the other seventeen-year-olds, they're dying. Our parents, everyone!" Matt said.

"Do you want to die trying to save them?" Justin asked.

"You don't care?" Matt asked.

"My parents were assholes," Justin said. "Good riddance."

"Look, let's just stay a few days." Darin said. "Let the snow melt, and we can reassess. You said Westbrook was crushed. How?"

CHAPTER 32

"The truck must have blown a tire," Matt said. "When he tried to pull the pods off the truck they fell off and crushed him. Luckily, he'd gotten Cody out first, before he was crushed."

"Where's the truck?" Darin asked.

"A little way up the road," Catherine said. "But it's totaled. The flood ruined it."

"So . . . we have no way to get there?" Darin asked. "I'm telling you, it's better here. Wherever here is."

"You seem a little too eager to stay and too happy about Dr. Westbrook's death," Matt said.

"Death is always sad. But trust me when I tell you, he wasn't well intended," Darin explained.

"How did you know he said that?" Matt asked.

"Because I filmed him for the better part of a decade. Sometimes he would send me on a task and would film while I was gone. He never let me see those recordings. I'm not saying he was evil, just troubled. Maybe it was the isolation. I don't know."

"What do we do?" Catherine asked. "Matt's right, we need to get back and pick up where Dr. Westbrook left off."

"Fine," Darin said. "But let's wait a few days. I need to regain some energy, and the snow needs to melt."

"No," Matt said. "I want to go now."

"Go where?" Darin asked. "I told you, I don't know how we got here. And I meant what I said. I'm not going back out there without a gas mask."

Darin padded toward the chairs and gingerly lowered himself. He hunched forward, resting his elbows on his knees. Victoria placed a can with a torn label in front of him with a mug of water. She paused but said nothing and sat next to him.

"Thank you," he said. "How many cabins are there?"

"I dunno," Cody said. "Probably a dozen or so. Plus, there are outbuildings."

"Maybe there are gas masks in one of them?" Darin asked. "Have you searched the place?"

"Briefly," Catherine said. "We were just looking for shoes and food. The cabins were pretty barren, but I suppose there could have been masks in one of them. I wasn't looking for that kind of thing."

"Me n-neither," Nathan said.

"I didn't see any," Stacy said. "Matt did most of the searching. Although I *did* find the trunk."

"Okay, then will you meet me halfway?" Darin asked. "Please, once the snow stops, let's search every building for masks. If we don't find any, then we'll come up with a plan B. I mean, look at me, I'm in no condition to even walk down the stairs. I just need a day or two to regain my strength. Being passed out for three days—it really messed me up.”

Matt opened his mouth and found himself at a loss.

“I’m not trying to not help,” Darin said. “I just want to do it right. What’s the point if we just end up dying in the apocalypse?”

“It’s snowing really hard again,” Stacy said. “I vote we wait like Lance—um, Darin—said. It really looks gross out there.”

“Fine.” Justin smirked. “It’s not like we have snow-shoes anyway.”

“Anyone opposed to this?” Matt crossed the room and held out a hand toward Darin. He shook it. “Then it’s a deal.”

CHAPTER 33

Matt spent the majority of the day staring out the window, willing the snow to stop. He overheard Stacy officially name Darin, Lance-Darin, which seemed to make Justin jealous. As much as Matt hated to admit it, Darin was right, and Matt's years of Scout training gnawed at him. *Scouts are always prepared.*

A hand on Matt's back startled him.

"You okay?" Catherine asked.

"Yeah," Matt said. "I'm just kicking myself. I should have searched the cabins better. Told everyone else to. No one should have been swimming when we could have been scouring the place for supplies."

"Matt, that's nuts. None of us could have known what was next. Honestly? It's been a lot the last few days. I think we could all use a day to just process everything."

"And just stand by when the entire human race could be dying?"

"Chill out, Matt." Catherine frowned. "Don't get mad at me. I want to find my parents as much as you—

we all do. Well, maybe not Justin. But what can we do? We are snowed in, and that's that. Try and give yourself a break. I found some Stephen King books in the game closet, you should grab one."

"You're right," he said. "I'm sorry."

"Ma-matt," Nathan interrupted. "It's getting pretty cold in here."

"I don't have any experience with fireplaces or what to look for," Matt said.

Justin sat in a chair, legs splayed out. "I do, chief." He sprang to his feet toward the hearth.

"Awesome," Stacy said. "Why didn't you say something before?"

"No one asked." He lay on his back and stared up into the chimney. "I didn't grow up rich like the rest of you. Burning wood was the only source of heat in our house. I know how to make a fire too. But you didn't ask me about that either, did you?"

"Sorry," Matt said.

"That I'm poor?" Justin's voice echoed. He stood and was fully inside the large fire box now, with his head up the chimney, only his lower legs exposed. "Don't be, we're all on the same level now. Hand me a broom or something."

"No, I'm sorry I didn't ask." Matt rubbed his hand over his buzzcut. "We're all still getting to know each other, so please speak up. I shouldn't have assumed no one had knowledge in this area."

"Here." Victoria crouched and angled a straw broom up the chimney.

"Thanks," Justin said.

Justin banged the broom so hard and loud inside the chimney that Matt wondered if Justin was smacking the bricks as if it was Matt's face.

"You doing okay in there?" Matt asked. "I really am sorry."

Justin emerged from the fireplace, face and hands smeared with soot. "No problem, chief. You know what they say about *assuming*. Everything looks clear. No nests or debris; we shouldn't smoke up the place. I'm going to get some firewood."

"Sounds like a plan," Cody said. "Count me in. I'm freezin'."

"I'll help," Catherine said. "I need some fresh air."

"M-me too," Nathan echoed.

"Have fun," Stacy said.

Just as they filed out, Stacy turned to Matt. "You shouldn't be so hard on him."

"Justin?" Matt furrowed his brow.

"Yeah. He seems like he's damaged. Had a hard life or something."

"I'm not! Are you *serious* right now? He's been the combative—you know . . . fine."

Matt stalked over to the theater stage, hoisted himself up and sat with his legs dangling. *This is ridiculous. How am I the bad guy all of a sudden?* He stared at the peeling varnish on the basketball court, lost in thought until he was smacked with a cold burst of air.

"How was it out there?" Victoria ran to the door and closed it behind Nathan, Cody, Catherine, and Justin. "Is it letting up?"

"Hell no!" Justin shook snow from his hair.

"Gettin' worse, actually," Cody said.

"Really?" Darin stood and walked to the window. On the third step, he collapsed.

"Lance-Darin, are you okay?" Stacy ran over and crouched next to him. "Justin, help me get Lance-Darin up."

"Easy, big fellah," Justin said, then lifted Darin.

"I want to see," Darin said.

"Okay, okay." Justin placed Darin's arm around his neck and acted as a crutch as they made their way to the window.

"No way we can travel in that," Darin said, shaking his head. "It's snowing sideways."

"Y-y-you're telling me," Nathan said. "I don't th-think anyone should go out alone. It's near whiteout conditions. Blizzard t-type weather."

Cody sat crouched next to the fireplace and struck the flint. Sparks landed on an old playbill he had wadded up for the starter. Soon the wood cackled and snapped, and flames danced in the fireplace.

Matt jumped down from the stage and walked over to the folding chairs. He grabbed them two at a time and set them up near the fire.

"Thanks for getting the wood," Matt said. "And Justin, it's awesome you knew how to check the chimney and stuff."

"Yep," Justin said. He deposited Darin in the chair closest to the fire. "You gonna be all right, man?"

"Yes," Darin said. "I think I just stood up too fast. I should be good as new tomorrow."

"Let's hope," Matt said.

Darin nodded and watched the flames.

It didn't take long to warm everyone, before the front door burst open and they were hit with another wave of bitter cold.

CHAPTER 34

"Um, like, hello?" Kim yelled.

Several feet of snow spilled in around her feet. Rhett pushed in behind her, then turned and tried to force the door shut.

"Kim!" Stacy ran to Kim and embraced her in a full hug. "It's so rude you just ditched me like that. I'm so glad you're okay."

"Sorry." Kim faked a frown.

"Glad you're back." Justin lifted his chin in Rhett's direction.

"Ran out of crap to burn," Rhett said. "Wait, is that . . ."

"Oh yeah, he woke up. *Finally*," Stacy said. "He says his name is Darin. But I call him Lance-Darin. You can too, if you want."

"I'll leave that to you," Kim said. "So what's your story, Darin? You getting us out of here or what?" She rocked back on her heels.

"You said you burned stuff," Darin started. "Did you come across any gas masks?"

"Uh, no. We only burned the furniture," Kim said. "And by we, I mean Rhett."

"Sorry." Rhett shrugged. "I didn't see any masks, and I searched the whole cabin pretty good. Why do we need gas masks?"

"Dang," Matt said.

"Come have a seat, and we'll fill you in," Victoria said. "How deep was the snow?"

"At least three feet," Rhett said. "I had to carry Kim."

"Just like the gentleman he is." Kim grinned ear to ear and sat next to Victoria.

Victoria proved to be an incredible storyteller and historian, as she recounted what had happened in perfect detail over a candlelit dinner of canned food and water.

"Guys, it's getting dark, I think we should sleep," Matt said.

"Looks like Darin beat you to it, chief," Justin said.

Darin slouched in the chair with his chin resting on his chest. An empty can of SpaghettiOs in a limp hand threatened to fall off his knee.

"He can use my sleeping bag," Kim said. "I'll share with Rhett."

"How nice of you." Catherine rolled her eyes.

"Hey, Lance-Darin!" Stacy shouted. "Get your lazy butt up and sleep in a bag, will ya?"

Matt laughed, still unable to get a pulse on the situation. Stacy either had a terrible way of flirting or outright hated this guy.

Darin seemed to be equally confused. He stood and

rubbed his eyes. Everyone else shuffled to their respective bags. Most moved theirs near the warm fire. Rhett and Kim didn't, though that didn't surprise Matt, since Rhett had declared himself a "hot sleeper."

Matt stared out the window at the massive mountain then had an idea. He turned and saw that everyone was asleep. It would have to wait until morning.

CHAPTER 35

Matt woke before the others and waited anxiously for everyone to wake. With his patience thin, he faked an overly loud sneeze. Cody was the first up and met Matt near the picture window.

"Dang, look at those drifts," Cody said. "I ain't never seen one that big before. Hey everyone, come look! There must be twelve-foot snowdrifts out there."

Snow had piled up in huge mounds across camp. Despite the continued snowfall, the brightness of the morning was amplified by the glittering white powder. The wind pattern must have shifted throughout the night, as the drifts were in varying directions.

"Wow," Catherine said. "The wind *was* fierce last night, kept waking me up."

"Me too," Justin said. "And you're welcome. I kept the fire going all night."

"Well, aren't you just turning out to be the best little helper?" Stacy teased, and tried to squeeze his cheek before getting her hand swatted away.

"Look, it's not that. I—I just realized that maybe this isn't the haven I thought it was," Justin said. "I mean, look outside. I'm with Matt now. I think we should look for the vault once it's safe to leave."

"How are you feeling, Darin?" Matt asked.

Darin stood and did a full-body stretch, complete with an audible yawn. "Not too bad."

"Like, that could take, like, months," Kim said.

"Or just a day," Victoria said. "Who knows?"

"M-maybe," Nathan said.

"Where you taking us, anyway?" Rhett asked.

"Like I've said, I don't know where to begin looking," Darin said. "And we must have gas masks. I don't want to put my lungs through that again."

"But you and Dr. Westbrook said the cryovault was inside a cave within a mountain, right?" Matt said.

"Yes." Darin tilted his head to the side, confused.

"What about that mountain?" Matt tapped on the window. The peak of the mountain jutted high into the sky. Yesterday the jagged rock was gray with a small cap of snow. Now the entire peak was solid white. The green trees below were blanketed with heavy snow. A winter wonderland worthy of Christmas morning. "I wonder how long it'll take to get there."

"I—I don't know, but when we left, the air was terrible." Darin walked to the window and shook his head. "I don't know how the air would clear so fast."

"Well, it was like 90 degrees yesterday—now look outside," Kim said.

"Y-y-yeah," Nathan said. "It flooded, and the water disappeared within an hour."

"So," Matt eagerly concluded, "since the weather changes so quick—you know, apocalypse and all—why couldn't the air change and become nontoxic just like that?" He snapped his fingers.

Darin tipped his head to one side, then rubbed his chin.

"So then you agree?" Matt said. "The air here is fine, so if we don't find gas masks we can go as far as that mountain and see if the vault is in there."

"I mean, I guess." Darin's lips were in a flat line, his jaw set. "But if it starts getting bad, I'm turning back."

"It is the only mountain in the vicinity," Cody added.

"You're the only one who knows how to run the cryopod systems. We need you. Please," Matt said.

"Yeah, Lance-Darin, stop being selfish," Stacy said. "I'd like to see my family again."

A chorus of "me toos" followed.

A small smile formed on Darin's lips. "Okay, once the snow lets up, we'll go. I relent. I was just worried about our safety, not trying to be selfish. Trust me, my intentions are good."

TO BE CONTINUED

BONUS CHAPTER FOR APOCALYPSE FALL,
BOOK # 2 IN THE SEASONS OF AN APOCALPYSE SERIES

CHAPTER 1

Matt Voorhees stared out the largest picture window in the main cabin of Camp New Beginnings. Outside was a picturesque winter wonderland worthy of a tacky gilded frame placed above the couch. If only he had a couch, and a home, and parents.

Well, technically, he *did* have parents. They were just cryogenically frozen inside a cave—somewhere. And hopefully still alive.

"Is the snow ever going to let up?" Matt crossed his arms over the Commodore 64 logo on his shirt. The roaring fireplace was nice, but it only really kept you warm if you were close. "This is ridiculous. It's probably snowed another foot."

"Better, like, watch out, Victoria," Kim said. "Much more snow, and it'll be deeper than you are tall."

"Very funny." Victoria stood with pin-straight posture and smoothed her long, black Gothic dress. "I'm not that short." She looked at her shoes.

"Chill out," Stacy said. "Besides, we have a bunch of buff guys here that can carry you—if the snow ever stops."

"I can manage myself," Victoria said. "Catherine, will you French braid my hair?"

"You should tease it up like Elvira and plop it on top of your head like this." Stacy gathered her frizzy strawberry-blond curls on top of her head. "It'll give you a few inches."

"Come on," Catherine motioned with her chin toward the hearth, "let's do it over here. You know I've never had my hair braided? It's too thick and curly."

"I can try after you do mine," Victoria said.

Catherine waddled toward the fireplace, holding up an oversized pair of gray sweatpants over her striped shorts. Most had just opted to use blankets, but a few layered on what they could find in the tattered trunk. Once they were closer to the crackling flames, Matt couldn't hear their conversation, but Victoria's shoulders relaxed and a small smile crept onto her pale face.

Cody sidled up to Matt and pressed his forehead against the window, leaving a greasy smudge.

"First time I saw snow in Texas, I thought it was neato burrito," Cody said. "Now it's the ugliest thing I done ever seen."

"No joke," Matt said. "It's so frustrating. We're stuck. Mother Nature wins again."

"How you feelin'?" Cody turned to Darin.

"Better. See?" Darin sprinted across the ragged gym floor toward Matt. His toe caught on warped wood, and he stumbled with flailing arms before regaining his footing. "I'm okay! I told you, I just needed a day to get myself right. I'm still not a hundred percent, but I'm getting there."

"Good. I'm glad." Matt stared back out at the flat gray sky, willing the sun to shine.

The only shirt large enough to fit Darin was a navy-blue polo with the word *Counselor* embroidered onto the left breast and a pair of too-short, pleated khaki shorts. Matt found a small bit of comfort in the counselor shirt. It seemed to tell everyone that Darin was in charge, and it took the pressure off him.

"Wh-what's the plan?" Nathan asked. He had a blanket slung over his shoulders. Only the *AS* was visible on his NASA shirt.

"I guess as soon as it stops snowing, we go," Matt said.

"No, not th-th-that." Nathan shifted his gaze to the floor. "The bodies."

"Right." Matt pinched the bridge of his nose. "Justin, you said you saw the bodies in the water?"

"What's that, chief?" Justin cupped his ear but made no attempt to come closer to Matt.

Matt rolled his eyes and walked toward Justin, Rhett, Stacy, and Kim. Cody, Nathan, and Darin followed behind Matt.

"You said you saw Dr. Westbrook and the girl, um, float by?" Matt asked.

"Yep." Justin shuffled a deck of cards. "They were pretty bloated too. Good job on burying them, Nathan."

"I'm so-sorry," Nathan said.

"Nah, I'm just giving you a hard time, bud," Justin said. "I wasn't exaggerating, though. They're pretty messed up."

"Sick!" Kim said. "That's, like, totally disgusting, and I won't listen to this. Come on, Rhett. Bring me a sleeping bag or something."

Kim turned on a heel. The pleats on her cheerleading skirt flashed blue and gold. Rhett shrugged and followed her toward the theater stage.

"We'll need to bury Kyle too. Pay our respects, you know." Cody gripped the spot where a rodeo belt buckle should have been and nodded at Matt.

"Yes, we'll do that first. Before we go to the mountain," Matt said.

"I thought you were in a big hurry," Darin said. "I'm not complaining, just saying."

"I'd like to get them buried before they . . . I can't even believe I'm saying this, but we probably should do it before they thaw out," Matt said.

"Th-three graves is a l-lot of work," Nathan said. "And we have to go deeper this time."

"Yes," Matt said. "All hands on deck this time."

"Or we could just do one big hole," Justin said.

"What?" Stacy gasped. "That's uncivilized."

"For once, I agree with you, Justin," Matt said.

"It does seem a little, I dunno, disrespectful," Cody said.

"Well, cowboy, we're fresh out of coffins and back-hoes," Justin said.

"I agree," Darin said. "You guys can put it to a vote if you'd like."

"No," Matt said. "It's not ideal, but it has to get done, and done quickly. They're rotting—we have no time to waste."

"Then it's settled," Justin said. "Pop a squat, let's play poker or rummy."

A loud gust of wind rattled the door. Matt secretly hoped it was someone coming to rescue them at the door, but he knew better. This was up to them.

* * *

Neither Matt nor Darin was in the mood to play cards. Plus, Justin was on Matt's side at the moment. He didn't want to sully the relationship by whipping him at rummy. He passed by Kim and Rhett on the stage. They lay facing each other with their legs intertwined. Kim brushed a lock of Rhett's blond hair off his forehead. They looked like Ken and Barbie. Only this Ken doll was six-six, with big blue eyes and a big, dumb brain. Kim whispered into Rhett's ear, and he laughed, then responded by tickling her.

"You think they ever get tired of playing tonsil hockey?" Matt asked, pointing his thumb toward them.

"Have they been like this the whole time?" Darin hoisted himself onto the stage next to Matt.

"Before, actually. They woke up on the bus ride to the cryovault. They say they didn't see anything because they were too busy doing that." He pointed at them. "Sick, man, just sick."

"Wait, are we sure they didn't see anything?" Darin asked. "Maybe they know where the vault is."

"We asked them a few times," Matt said. "Trust me, we got more details than I cared to hear, but nothing useful. Ah, here we are."

Matt did his best Vanna White impression and presented the tapes to Darin. Eighteen black rectangular halves and the spools lay splayed out on a *Gremlins* beach towel. Small screws and three screwdrivers lay amongst the organized chaos.

"I hope these still work," Matt said.

"Me too," Darin said. "Good idea on taking them apart to dry out."

"Thanks. I accidentally spilled water on my mom's new Debbi Gibson cassette once and used this same method to dry it out. The case cracked a little, but it still worked," Matt said. He tightened the tape on the reels, then carefully placed the backpiece over it. "Hand me a Phillips, will ya? I like the orange-handled one best."

"Trav's Auto Care," Darin said, examining the screwdriver. His face darkened. "I'm here. Alive and breathing. Whoever this Trav was, he isn't. Gone. Dead. Like everyone else in the world. It's kind of surreal when you think about it."

"Yeah," Matt said. He took the tool from Darin and slowly replaced the screws. "It makes me wonder how and why we were picked."

"Me too," Darin said, bowing his head. "Me too."

"You know, with all the snow, it's too bad we can't go sledding." Matt changed the subject.

"I haven't been sledding since I was a kid." Darin laughed. "We could use the canoe."

"My parents drove me to Tahoe a few times with our dog. He was a Chesapeake Bay Retriever. You know what they look like?"

"No. I'm not a big fan of dogs," Darin said.

"What? How is that even possible? Dogs truly are a man's best friend."

"Not when they're chasing you," Darin said. "I used to deliver papers."

"A paperboy?" Matt laughed.

"Hey, I was only twelve when I was frozen, remember? Anyway, a few would chase me relentlessly. I got bitten once. It scared me."

Statements like that were odd to Matt. Darin had been put in cryosleep just like them, but he'd awakened for nearly a decade before he was forced back to sleep. Actual time had passed for him. He'd aged.

"Saber wouldn't have done that," Matt said.

"You named your dog Saber?"

"Yep." Matt beamed. "I love movies. *Star Wars* is one of my favorites. Anyway, Saber loved the snow. I grew up in Nevada, so we had to drive to the mountains to see snow. Saber would ride on the sled with me, all eighty pounds of him. We'd fly down those hills. It's one of my favorite memories."

Matt's voice cracked, and his eyes filled with tears. He turned away from Darin and wiped his eyes.

"You really liked that dog, huh?" Darin asked.

"It's not that." Matt cleared his throat. "It's every-thing. I need to make sure my family is okay. And after that, I want to rebuild. Have a dog again. Live normal. Not eat expired canned food. And none of that can happen while the sky vomits snow all over us."

"I know," Darin said. "We all do. Well, maybe not those two." He pointed to Rhett and Kim. "They're about three seconds away from actually *showing* us how babies are made. Hey! You two cover up or get a room!"

Matt laughed and dried his eyes one more time. "I think this tape will work." He used his index finger to spin the reels. "Cody, can you fire up the gennie?"

As a kid, Tyler H. Jolley always had a knack for storytelling. When he grew bored of old fables, he created his own exciting and unique worlds. Many years later, he still had so many new ideas and stories swirling in his head, but with nowhere to share it. That's when he put his pencil to paper and let the creative juices flow.

His debut novel, EXTRACTED, came out in 2013 and swiftly became an Amazon Best Seller and Spencer Hill Press Best Seller. PRODIGAL AND RIVEN, the second and third books in The Lost Imperials series were released in May of 2015.

After a brief hiatus he restructured and returned to writing. His Adventurous Ali series has received much praise. To date, he's released three in the series.

When he's not writing, you can find him at his orthodontic practice, mountain biking, or on the hunt for the perfect doughnut.